MW01193748

Centralia, PA Devils Fire

By: Andrew Shecktor

A fictional novel based on actual events surrounding the underground coal mine fire in Centralia, PA which began around Memorial Day, 1962

This novel is a fiction based on actual events. Many of the events actually occurred, but this is not to state that this is anything other than fictional. Names have been changed from historical characters when depicted as fiction and characters and events have been added that are purely fictional. Any similarity of events or characters is purely coincidental.

Centralia, PA
Devils Fire

By: Andrew Shecktor
CR 2014 Shecktor Enterprises, Inc.
All rights reserved
Printed in the United States

About the Author

Born in 1956 in Philadelphia, and currently residing in Berwick Pennsylvania in the heart of coal country, Andrew Shecktor has authored a number of short manuscripts and articles of fiction and non-fiction over his 40 year part time writing career. He worked as a technical writer for ECRI, a medical device evaluation firm in Plymouth Meeting, PA. He assisted his mother, Maria C. Shecktor (deceased), published author of children's books, with her adult class on creative writing. She has been his inspiration for his writings and for the writing of this novel. Mr. Shecktor draws upon many years of diversified experience from world travel to participation in many religious traditions (primarily as a learning experience.) He is a self-taught fine artist in oil, acrylic and pastel, and is a member of the North Mountain Art League. He is also an amateur photographer, an art he learned from his father, Fred Kerek Shecktor (deceased), who was the public relations director for the city of Philadelphia in the 1960's. Fred worked for Ed Bacon, director of the Philadelphia City Planning Commission and father of actor Kevin Bacon. The author had the pleasure of going on several hunting trips with Ed and Kevin (and an assortment of other Philadelphia dignitaries) in the northern tier of Pennsylvania. On these trips he would pass twice through Centralia. Once on the way up and once on the way back. He got to see the town first hand before the fire had progressed, up to the point of the fire being of serious concern to the residents.

The author is an electrical engineer by trade and has worked as a biomedical equipment engineer in charge of several major city hospitals. Recently he has worked in the computer industry and website services. He has also been involved in the political arena both as support staff and as a candidate for office. He has a keen interest in ghost hunting and the study of scientific anomalies, believing, ahead of his time, in the idea of quantum oddities. In his own words, "We are in general extremely narrow minded. We think that ours is the one real and true reality. Our science is accurate and cannot be displaced. In fact, we are wrong. There is far more to this world and this universe than our tiny minds will ever be able to conceive. Our science is based on that narrow spectrum of knowledge which we are permitted to see and touch with our hands and our instruments. We search for alien radio waves, yet why would aliens communicate using radio waves, when communication could be instantaneous via quantum or other techniques which we cannot yet even begin to conceive. We view ourselves as solid beings and our world as being the same, when in fact the more you magnify a person, a rock, or even the air; the smaller you look, the more you will find that we are really nothing but energy and empty space. There is really no such thing as matter. Could there not be other beings that differ significantly from us? Perhaps even beings of pure energy. Perhaps there are indeed gods and demons and even other universes filled with beings far different than us that interact with the universe and perceive the universe differently from us."

It is the author's varied personal experiences, open mind, knowledge and knack for research, which combine to bring plausibility to even the oddest fictional story. This story is a unique attempt to combine historical fact with fiction. The story amplifies several tales of myth and legend that have been handed down through time, and works them into the actual history of the town of Centralia, PA. The author envisions this as a way to pique the reader's interest to research the history further. He plans on writing similar works on other small town myths if this format goes over well.

Preface

Centralia, PA -The True Story

Centralia, PA is located in northeast Pennsylvania, in the heart of the coal mining region. The zip code, 17927, was abandoned following the buyout of all but a handful of properties in the aftermath of a devastating mine fire that is believed to have begun just before Memorial Day, 1962.

The land which was to become Centralia was purchased from local Native American tribes in 1749 for the sum of five hundred pounds (over $800,000 in today's money.)

In 1793 Robert Morris, a Declaration of Independence signer, acquired about a third of the area which later became Centralia. He later went bankrupt and his land went to Bank of the United States.

Jonathan Faust opened the Bull's Head Tavern in 1832. In 1842 Centralia's land was bought by the Locust Mountain Coal and Iron Company, and Alexander Rae, a mining engineer, created the village and named it "Centreville," which was changed a year later to "Centralia" because Schuylkill County already had a town named "Centreville."

The coal deposits were pretty much ignored until the Mine Run Railroad was constructed in 1854. The mine Run Railroad was built to transport coal out of the nearby valley.

The first two coal mines opened in 1856, the Locust Run Mine and the Coal Ridge Mine. Others followed in the 1860's.

Evil had hold of the town from the beginning, with fights among miners over coal vein mining rights, fights among mine bosses, and local residents looking for land to settle. Then there were the infamous "Molly Maguires", one of the most violent crime families of the time. A group of primarily Irish mine workers, their intent was honorable and sincere; to ensure fair wages and a safe working environment for all workers, but their methods were sometimes despicable. They would not hesitate for a moment to murder an offending mine boss or mine owner, in the name of their cause. Most of their leaders were hanged in Bloomsburg in 1877, but some of their descendants may have survived into the 1980's according to legend.

Alexander Rae, the town's founder, was murdered by the Maguires in his buggy while en route to Mount Carmel from Centralia in 1868. The Maguires were also responsible for a string of murders and violence across the region, most notably in Mauch Chunk (present day "Jim

Thorpe"). Unlike other gangs, the Maguires mainly pillaged for the fun of it – rarely was there a reason for their violence, despite their claiming to be vigilantes fighting for workers rights.

At its peak, around 1890, the town had seven churches, five hotels, a bank, a post office, 14 stores and a population of 2,761. Coal production declined during World War 1 due to the loss of manpower to the war, and again dwindled during the Great Depression. A number of mines were closed during the Great Depression due to the inability to sell their product, and more closed during World War II due to the scarcity of workers, many having been sent off to war. In addition, after World War II oil and gas began taking over many of the roles of coal.

There was a small mine fire in 1931 that some say never fully went out and which may have rekindled and started the underground mine fire that ultimately led to the town being declared uninhabitable, after which the town was taken over by the state by eminent domain. It is, however, more probable that it was the intentional burning of rubbish in a landfill pit, formerly a strip mine and thought to have been sealed, near the Odd Fellows cemetery, which caused the fire to ignite the coal vein on May 27, 1962. This fire was set at the request of the town council to clean up the town in preparation for the Memorial Day holiday, one of the most important holidays in town, and one of the few holidays that was given to virtually all "non-essential" personnel. The fire re-kindled on a number of occasions during that year, and the Lehigh Valley Coal Company and Pennsylvania Bureau of Mine Safety became involved. In any event, the coal fire spread, and over the course of the next two decades many parts of Centralia and adjacent Byrnesville were affected by the fire.

The fire was thought to be extinguished until 1979 when John Coddington, a local gas station owner (later to be one of Centralia's Mayors) discovered that his station's underground gas tanks were reading a dangerously high temperature of 172 degrees Fahrenheit. In addition, a number of residents noted that in the winter they no longer had to shovel the snow that fell, as it melted quickly by itself due to the earth being heated by the fire.

Centralia came into the national news on Valentine's Day, 1981 when 12 year old Todd Domboski, who was working on a motorcycle near his grandmother's home, noticed a wisp of smoke coming from the ground not far off. He went over to investigate and was consumed by a four foot wide, 150 foot deep sinkhole. He grabbed onto some roots to stop his fall. Acrid smoke arose all around him. Passerby heard his screams for help and pulled him from the abyss.

By 1986 most of the town's homes had been condemned by the state and by 2003 most of the homes were bought under eminent domain and were razed, and the area was declared unfit for habitation. A few residents refused to leave and filed a legal action. They won the legal action in 2013 and will be allowed to remain until their deaths, after which their homes will become the property of the state.

There are many great books and articles and documentaries on the Centralia mine fire. This is but a sampling of the history to serve as point of reference for the fictional novel which follows. Much of the most interesting history has unfortunately been lost to time, between the official shutdown of the town and the fact that historical records of most small rural towns has been considered inconsequential, with only the most notable or important facts being retained. In addition, it has been rumored that many historical records were destroyed intentionally to cover up questionable activity, perhaps to cover up the mine companies attempts to obtain the town's mineral rights. As there was no Internet or computer storage in those days, all records were on paper. Many paper records were only kept for so long, after which they were destroyed.

Some say there never was a danger from the fire (save for a small area of town), and that the town is to this day habitable, noting that once the last resident leaves, the town land becomes the property of the state and can be given to the coal miners to strip mine, something they could not do with the town residing on the land. Below

Centralia remain some of the richest anthracite coal deposits in Pennsylvania. The town had acquired the mineral rights in 1950 under a law enacted in 1949 that allowed them to do so. Oddly, Centralia was the only Pennsylvania municipality to do so. In some other municipalities, the residents were forcibly evicted from their homes when the mine operators decided to strip mine under the town. Neither those towns nor the residents owned the mineral rights.

Legend has it that Father Ignatius McDermott, the first Roman Catholic priest to call Centralia home, cursed the land in retaliation for being assaulted by three members of the Molly Maguires in 1869. McDermott said that "there would be a day when St. Ignatius Roman Catholic Church would be the only structure remaining in Centralia."

In 2016 many of the former residents will be returning to their home town for the 50th anniversary of a time capsule they placed. They will be returning to a town with no fire, and also no homes or businesses.

Mining company conspiracy to shut the town down to strip mine it, unfortunate accident caused by careless burning, or a curse from a powerful Roman Catholic priest. You decide.

Forward

The story which follows is a fictitious accounting; based on fact, of the history of the underground mine fire in Centralia, PA, which most likely started around Memorial Day, 1962 and continues burning to this day. It is based on actual historical events and an actual trip by the author to present day Centralia, as well as other local mining towns. Much research has been done to ensure that the framework of this novel is historically correct. Most names, other than those that are historical and based on fact, have been changed, and some characters have been added to enhance the story.

Although most dates and other information on Centralia are based on fact, this entire work should be considered fictional.

During the research for this novel the more I investigated, the more I found that the actual history of the town is almost more interesting and unusual than the story I planned to weave. I have not included any of the mine company issues or the issues surrounding the mineral rights being obtained by the town. Volumes of fascinating history could be written on this alone. I also found that it is extremely difficult to locate information on the town prior to 1962. Even the genealogical libraries and historical societies appear lean on this information. And, if you search the Internet for information on the mine fire all you find is the same canned stuff that the state has put out, reproduced pretty much verbatim. Most of the old-timers are reluctant to discuss the history of the fire as well, since the manner in which the landfill fires were started was controversial, and most want to put the past behind them. There are also a number of different theories on how the fire started, from a rekindle of a fire that occurred in 1931 to a non-related trash fire to a possible re-kindle of the landfill fire due to the warm temperatures that summer. Many attempts to put the fire out were undertaken, most were under-funded and thus failed. Did the mining companies really want the fire to go out, or did they want the state to take over the town by eminent domain so they could gain the mineral mines to strip mine the town? Many of the answers to these questions we may never know, but there certainly is opportunity for a well researched treatise on the town and its history and on the history of the mine fire that destroyed the town and the attempts to put it out.

When you walk around what once was the town of Centralia you see only a very few areas that have been affected by the fire. The fire is still burning, and will probably continue to burn for a hundred years, or more, but it has moved on. It is truly sad that this town ceased to exist when such a small area was affected. But there is one shining light. On August 28, 2011 the Blessed Virgin

Mary Church celebrated 100 years of worship. This church remained because it is located on the north hill overlooking the town, and is far enough away that it was not affected by the mine fire. It is truly wonderful to see this church, standing out amidst that majestic hill.

Despite being forewarned to avoid the area due to the dangers of underground collapse, it is worth a visit to the site. It is truly amazing to see the streets with no homes, not even a single foundation. Not a driveway or a curb. Yet roads to nowhere and utility poles still remain. Just how was all of that removed, and why? It is not like it was capped or back-filled, just gone! It is as if aliens came in a spaceship and just transported all the homes and businesses off the planet. Then there is old Route 61 – the road to nowhere, closed down long ago. Covered with the endless writings of thousands of visitors and former residents it sits as a textbook in cement. I am sure your visit will be as provocative as was ours. Just beware the Gatekeeper, and enjoy your stay! Maybe you will even get to meet the old man with the pipe!

Chapter 1

Centralia, PA June 25, 1962

"More water! More water damn it! The fire is spreading!" From behind a fire pumper a soot covered black-faced fireman came running and shouting. "Around the other side! Quickly!"

Three more fire fighters joined in, sweat pouring from their brows in the 83 degree heat, made many times hotter by the raging fire, dragging limp cloth hose toward the quickly spreading fire that was reaching out in anger from the pit. "Charge the line," screamed a scrawny teenage fireman. The hose they were carrying quickly filled and whipped along like a disturbed snake.

The fire, in the pit of an old abandoned strip mine near the Odd Fellows cemetery was started once or twice a year to burn excess municipal rubbish, but had never gotten out of control, as did this one. This fire was started on May 27 to clean up rubbish and municipal waste in preparation for the Memorial Day celebration, and was then extinguished by the fire department and was thought to have gone out. It had again re-kindled on May 29 and was put out late in the evening. It again re-kindled on June 12, though not as bad. Now it had re-kindled yet again, this time with a vengeance, as if set by Satan himself. None of the locals had ever seen such an inferno. This was no ordinary fire. The flames leaping from the ground formed shapes resembling demons from Hell; the heat was melting fire apparatus staged many hundreds of feet from the pit.

A huge flame leaped from the pit. It displayed arms reaching toward the ground and had what looked like a wicked smirk on what seemed to be a fiery red face. It hissed and spat loudly, throwing sparks hundreds of yards. There was a loud "whoosh" and a bang, and it was sucked back into the pit. The earth rumbled deeply from below. The rumbling became louder, an ominous warning of that which was yet to come.

A nun from the local Catholic Church clutched her rosary and prayed, "Lord God, save us from the evil we have unleashed!"

Out of the burning abyss came a thunderous roar, a fiery black belch like a volcano and smelling putrid of sulfur. Dust and burning ash rained down from above. A black visage, vaguely visible through the smoke, floated in the air uttering evil in unknown tongues. Brilliant red flames in the shape of evil demons issued forth from the pit; their burning forked red tongues whipping wildly to and fro. A low pitched but quite perceivable reverberation could be heard warning, "Doomed! Doomed! You are all doomed!"

A blazing tail of fire roared from the pit and grabbed onto a police vehicle and two bystanders, dragging them screaming, slowly back into the pit with it, gone forever into the flaming abyss.

In the distance the din of rhythmic drumming, and the monotone sound of a group of 13 women could be heard chanting, "Guardians of the watchtower of the east, we do summon, stir and call thee to protect us in our rite. Come to us now on the cool breath of autumn's sigh which heralds the advent of winter and the close of harvest time. Breathe into us the spirit of the pure joy of life. So mote it be!"

There came another blast from the pit and the ground collapsed beneath a fire truck, sucking it down into the very bowels of hell, the ground closing over the vehicle and entombing it.

The circle continued, "Guardians of the watchtower of the south, we do summon, stir and call thee to protect us in our rite. Come forth from the cook fires and smokehouses where food is being made ready for the coming cold months. Kindle within us the flame of spiritual awakening. So mote it be!"

"Get back! Get back!" screamed a local police officer. "Move the perimeter back!!"

Quickly the entourage of fire fighters and borough workers gathered their equipment, leaving behind the hose they had already laid, and pulled back to a safe distance. Local police circled the area keeping bystanders out of view of the inferno. The ground where they had been collapsed and all the equipment that had been left behind was swallowed by the earth.

The circle of 13, who had been called in to close the gates continued chanting and drumming, not missing a single beat, all the while moving more distant from the flaming hole.

Chapter 2 – Road Trip!

Sunday, September 29, 2013 Berwick, PA

2013, the first year of the second term of Barack Obama, the first black U.S. President; the year of the implementation of the "Affordable Health Care Act," sometimes known as "Obamacare" or the "Unaffordable Health Care Act". The year that athlete Lance Armstrong lost his titles by admitting to drug enhancement doping; and the year that 85 year old Pope Benedict XVI resigned, shocking those of the Catholic Faith around the world. It was also a year in which there were an unprecedented number of random shootings, in schools and on military bases across the U.S and the world. More shocking, it was the year that my son, John, actually made the 120 mile trip, of his own volition, to visit his dad, and to tour the now virtually vacant town of Centralia.

"Hey Dad! It's John on the phone for you!" My daughter, Anna had answered the house phone, which rarely rings any more these days. Usually it is the cell phone, and most often it is a text that comes through.

"I've got it!" I shouted back, slowly making my way to the old desk phone.

I had moved to Berwick in northeast Pennsylvania from a suburb of Philadelphia over 8 years ago, taking with me only my wife and youngest daughter, Anna, to be closer to work. The other four siblings were all settled and did not have any desire to "move to the sticks". I, on the other hand, had a burning desire to get away from the congestion of the city, the noise and the high cost of living. Three of the siblings made a home together, with John being the dominant sibling, and lease holder of a nice suburban three bedroom home. John only rarely called though, unless he had a pressing need for help or required information on some obscure topic that could not be easily located.

I brushed the dust off the phone and picked it up. "Hey John, to what do I owe the pleasure?"

"Well dad," replied John, "me and Tyler are coming up to see Centralia – thought we might stop by since we'll be in the area."

"Sure! I'd love to see you, when will you be over?" It was around noon and we were just finishing lunch. John would have about a two hour drive and I figured there would be plenty of time to clean up and do the few chores that needed to be done. Tyler, John's best friend was always a bit slow getting moving too, usually need to set off a couple of firecrackers beside him to get him up, so I figured that would buy me a bit more time as well. John said they would be leaving right away. I finished cleaning the dishes and settled back with a cup of strong coffee.

At about 2 o'clock the doorbell rang – it was John and Tyler. I was unaware that they were coming here first and planned to take me along for the ride.

"Ready to rock and roll?" John asked excitedly.

Always one for an adventure, I grabbed my cameras, a notepad and pens and a snack for the road, and hopped in John's truck with Anna in tow. Anna was not one to be left out of a new adventure either.

John asked, "Ever been to Centralia since you moved up here?"

"Never been there, but we pass by it all the time on our way to other places," I answered. "You used to be able to see the smoke from the top of the hill at the Pioneer Tunnel Coal Mine in Ashland, but of late the skies seem pretty clear. Hope you're not too disappointed if we don't find much."

It was about a 45 minute drive to Centralia, and the time went fast. We made a stop for snacks and drinks along the way, and John topped off the fuel tank in his truck. John was big on big trucks, which unfortunately came along with really big fuel cost. John didn't care; I suppose he considered it a rite of passage. He wouldn't trade that big old truck for any other vehicle.

Along the way there were discussions of mining and ghost towns, and of what sparked the sudden interest in Centralia. Centralia was once a bustling town of around 2,000 plus souls, most of whom made a living blasting coal from the many mines around town. Most of the mining had ceased by the time the mine fire started just a couple of days before Memorial Day, 1962. It is most commonly believed that the fire in the abandoned mine shaft was ignited by a rubbish fire intentionally set by the fire department at the request of the borough council. The fires were set periodically to burn municipal waste. The fire was thought to have been put out that year, but in fact had smoldered and gone underground into the coal mine shafts to make itself known some 10 years later when the owner of a gas station noticed exceedingly high temperatures in his fuel tanks. The fire is still burning to this day, and could continue to burn for another hundred years or more. All but a handful of residents remain, being allowed to stay until their deaths or they move away by choice, after which their homes too will be destroyed and vanish forever.

We snaked through Bloomsburg, and then south through Catawissa, where we turned off to head for Centralia, taking the same route we had taken many times to visit the Pioneer Tunnel Coal Mine. It is also the same route I had taken that year to bring my car to a friend who is a mechanic and who has a garage in Mount Carmel, just to the west of Centralia.

Now, just ahead of us was what remained of the nearly vacant town. I suggested pulling into one of the long abandoned streets, parking and then hiking from there. It is really hard to follow the old maps when all the landmarks are gone, and it was equally hard to find an old map of Centralia on short order. The GPS was useless in this regard. As far as it was concerned we had arrived at a vacant field.

After taking a short tour of some of the streets, John parked the truck and we all got out to have a closer look and get our bearings. It was so odd, all of the streets leading to nowhere. It was as if beyond the dead ends and the sea of grass and trees there lay homes, and playgrounds, and stores invisible to us, but existing in another reality.

We started off on foot, following the road. The streets were in better shape than some of those in Berwick and aside from being blocked by debris to keep cars from going in too far, looked much like the streets of any well kept small town. The streets led to driveway cutouts, with no driveways. There were no houses and no signs of even the foundations of any of the homes, not even any construction or demolition debris. Utility poles with long disconnected wires lined the streets. We saw no smoke, no homes, no people except for an occasional visitor looking for the mine fire. We lost John and Tyler for a time. Both are tall and have long legs and a very long stride which made it difficult for me and Anna to keep up. I am considerably shorter than them, and Anna clocks in at just under 5 feet tall. Occasionally they would look back and see us in the distance and would sit on the ground and wait for us to catch up. We walked for what seemed an eternity and then came upon a barren area. The soil was cracked open and wisps of acrid gray smoke rose from the ground. We took lots of pictures and reveled at having found the smoke we were in search of! The ground was warm and gave off a smell of sulfur and rotten eggs. There were pipes protruding from the ground with warnings of the danger of toxic gases. Another pipe sticking up with a concrete barrier around it sported a sign warning tour buses to not back over the pipe. This was to be all the smoke we would see on our trip, but yet to come were far more interesting and unusual things.

After a short time we passed the gates to the Saints Peter and Paul cemetery. It appeared as any other cemetery, but it was odd in that there was no sign of the mine fire. The grass was green and well kept, and an American flag in pristine condition hung on the right gate pole. The gravestones were all standing tall and were as clean as the day they were laid. Some had flowers by them, others small flags. One had a small pink stuffed bunny beside it.

We continued on, still looking for the supposedly still burning mine fire. We came to see some smoke and the cracks in the earth, but save for the one small area of desolation with a couple of smoking and warm potholes; there was no carnage to be seen. Maybe the old tales about the mine companies wanting eminent domain of the town so they could strip mine it were accurate. Maybe there never was any real threat to the town, aside from a small area where the fire began.

About a mile into our journey we came upon another well kept cemetery, the cemetery of the St. Ignatius Roman Catholic Church. The main gate was wide open and the neatly preened grass was azure green. A massive lock and chain hung limply from the open gate. There was no sign that the mine fire had ever come near this place either. Even the squirrels and rabbits were bounding happily around this small oasis, playing merrily and chasing one another. Beautiful birds of all colors wafted overhead, landing on occasion to pick something tasty from the ground and then returning to flight. A cool breeze was blowing from the west, and the trees were swaying softly. Guarding the entrance was the granite gravestone of "Reverend Anthony P. Kane, Born December 9, 1910, Ordained June 15, 1955, Died November 9, 1986." Below which were the words "Thou art a priest forever". The grave of his parents lay to the left of his. Then we saw a stone marked "Brennan", beneath which read "Thomas E. 1894-

1956". To the right and below were "Margaret M. and Thomas Jr.". We paused wondering if these two souls were still alive, or perhaps were buried in another town, one not on fire. We then looked around at the beauty of the cemetery and wondered what had spared this patch of land? Is it guarded by the spirits of those long dead souls lying beneath the earth? Who is the caretaker? We took some more photos and tarried on.

A young couple approached us just as we were leaving the cemetery. "Where is the highway?" asked the woman. "Where is the old Route 61? We were told that it is the coolest place – we just have to find it!" I told her I wasn't sure, that this was our first time to the area as well. They showed us a tattered bit of paper with some crude directions and a hand drawn map. Based on what we had seen thus far we suggested a general direction in which the deserted highway may be and we went our separate ways.

Down a dusty, winding dirt road we went during which time several noisy 4-wheelers and dirt bikes sped past, carrying seedy looking characters I hoped we would not have the pleasure of meeting again. One whizzed by, engine roaring and popping, doing doughnuts in the dirt, throwing stones and dust in our direction. Obviously way too much testosterone. An elderly couple, both leaning on crooked canes, way too short to be of any structural value, past us heading in the other direction, back towards the St.

Ignatius church. Then we came upon a narrow opening in the trees. Peering through the majestic arch the two huge trees formed we saw the highway, the old route 61 that had been shutdown and bypassed years ago because the underground mine fire had damaged it, and the ground beneath it had become weakened due the now displaced coal that left huge weakened underground caverns, placing the roadway in jeopardy of collapse at any time.

We passed through the majestic arch formed by the two trees and cautiously approached the road. What we saw was unbelievable, more fascinating than we had imagined and way better than seeing smoke. The long closed road, cracked and pitted along its length, was covered with the graffiti of 50 years of visitors. The first icon we saw was a heart in which was written "Rest in Peace, Centralia". There were scores of crude and vulgar images, and sayings heard not even in the most seedy tavern in town. Mile after mile we traveled, every inch of road covered with these images. Written in white paint across a narrow crack in the road was scrawled "RIP Centralia". Then there were those who signed their names, Erich, Dawn, Justin, Adam and Kevin, printed next to a drawing of an Easter bunny, below which was written "Happy Easter from Silent Hill 2012". More dirt bikes and 4 wheelers passed. Then an old pickup truck, with more gaping holes, rust and auto putty than steel covering its' tattered frame, sped past, roaring like a mad lion as its' exhaust past freely into the air without the benefit of a muffler to quiet it. It belched black smoke from its tailpipe, temporarily obscuring our view. When the air cleared my attention was drawn to a pentagram on the road, around which was inscribed "Ego sum quis ego mos". Hmmm, "I am who I will". Must have missed something in Latin class. And then a smoke breathing turtle. I wonder what that represents?

The writings became older, some from the 1990's, just shortly after the road had been closed. Some told of love, some of hate, others of sorrow. A teddy bear with initials on either side. Santa Clause. Demons in red with vile forked tongues. I became overcome with sorrow myself. I was slowly learning about those who were forced to leave this wonderful small town. The writings forever etched in this street painted a sad tale of the end of a town which died a very slow and painful death. A town now lost forever to the sands of time.

The road started becoming more covered with overgrowth when we came upon the icon shown proudly in every book about the mining disaster, every website and every documentary made on the subject – the gaping cracks from which once poured mountains of thick gray-black smoke. But alas, the smoke had long gone back into the earth, though the ground was still slightly warm to the touch. This, we thought, would be the end of our journey, as we needed time to return to our vehicle before the sun dipped below the horizon forcing us to return in the dark.

That is when we saw him. An old gnarly fellow, perhaps in his late seventies, sporting a tattered casual sport coat with a torn vest pocket from which protruded a tattered handkerchief. He had on faded blue jeans and shoes with holes through which his toes shown. A felt hat, flattened from age, adorned his head. A pipe, charred and pitted from years of use, which he held securely between his teeth was billowing curly wisps of gray smoke. He was happily seated upon a large moss covered rock. He motioned to us with one outstretched finger to come nearer. He appeared relatively harmless, but considering some of the other characters we had come upon on our journey we approached with caution.

"You folks want to know the true story of this God forsaken place and of the mine fire?" he inquired. "Come sit and keep an old man company for a few minutes, and you will learn the truth from an old timer who has seen it first hand and who has heard all the tales from the past."

Curiosity got the better of us and we made ourselves comfortable on the ground while the old man told us of the Native Americans who sold the land that became Centralia to the first residents, how the town was built around the railroad that carried the coal from the valleys, and how the town was built on top of one of the richest coal seams in the area, with the mining companies always trying to gain control and close the town down so they could strip mine the land. He explained how the mine operators were responsible for pulling enough coal to meet the ever increasing quotas set by the mine owners, determined by the ever increasing demands of industry and electrical power generation. He told us of all the miners, some very young men and boys, who died in the terrible conditions under the earth. He told how mules lived their lives underground and were used to pull the coal sleds loaded down with their black treasure to the surface. We humored him, having already heard all of this from our many coal mine visits. He had, however, a sincere and pleasing tone of voice that could be listened to for eternity.

The old man paused, picked up his pipe, and breathed its dying embers back to life. Smoke snaked around his head slowly as it dispersed upward. "You know," the old man began, "life was good here until the Maguires came to town. Them people was bad news – caused a raucous down in Mauch Chunk, then came up this-a-way. Meanest bunch of brutes this side of the Mississippi. They killed the founder of our town, Alexander Rae, in cold blood in his buggy while he was coming from Mount Carmel one day in 1868. Then they made the mistake of giving a beating to Father Daniel Ignatius McDermott, the first Roman Catholic priest in town. The preacher got so mad his first day back to church he stood before his congregation and said that he cursed the Molly Maguires, the town of Centralia and the very land beneath them, commanding God to destroy these wretched hoodlums and rend the town destitute and barren. He swore that one day the St. Ignatius Roman Catholic Church would be the only remaining structure in town, and that there would be no people living here."

The old man paused again, peered toward the west where the sun was getting ready for bed, sparked a bit more smoke from his pipe and continued. "Most of the Maguires was hanged in Bloom in '87 afore the turn of the century, but some say their descendants lived on until the 1980's. Anyways, the coal started running dry by around 1900 and the mine owners was really mad. Beat the miners and mine operators – demanded they find where that black gold went. Seems that preachers curse was really working. About this time there were over 1000 folks living in town, lots of stores and houses of ill repute, and even more watering holes. More miners got a beating in them watering holes than in the mines it seems, mostly arguing over women, money or mine rights. Was never a dull night around here I am told."

Fear came upon his face. He tapped out the spent leaves from his pipe, pulled a ragged leather pouch from his vest pocket, and re-loaded the bowl. He pulled a match from his other pocket, struck it upon the rock on which he was sitting, and paused until the flame was about to consume his fingers. He slowly sucked the flame from the match into his pipe and a smile curled around his lips as the pipe came back to life. "You know, this town was doing pretty good until that preachers curse came true and all the coal veins dried up. One mine operator got greedy and decided to try and counteract the curse with one of his own and conjured up something so evil it would destroy this town." His eyes became dull and he looked toward the sky. "There weren't no putting this thing back in the bottle! But it all began with this vindictive preacher seeking personal satisfaction, demanding un-holy intervention on his behalf."

A light breeze blew from the west. The trees chanted eerily, their branches waving to and fro in tandem, as though they were aware of the unearthly story about to be told.

Thus began the old man's tale.

Chapter 3

The Curse – Centralia, PA Summer 1869

"A cosey seat
A dainty treat
Make Phoebe's
Happiness complete.
With linen white
And silver bright
Upon the Road
Of Anthracite"

(Lackawanna Railroad advertisement)

* * * * * * * * * * *

Burning Coal Mine

A Loss of $200,000 Caused By A Fire In A Coal Vein At Centralia.

Centralia, Penn., July 16.-The vein of coal at Provost Colliery is still burning fiercely together with the dirt and rock banks. The mine is being flooded now, but with poor prospects of overcoming the flames, which gained considerable headway during the night, and are now endangering the workings of the Continental and Hazel Dell Mines, which are only divided from the burning vein by a pillar of coal 30 feet thick. Should the workings take fire this town would be ruined. Several valuable pumping engines were destroyed, together with the breaker, office, and all buildings except the stables. The loss is estimated this morning at $200,000. The breaker was insured with Provost and Herring, of Philadelphia, but to what amount is not known here. Just before the fire commenced a car-load of miners, who were descending into the pit, made a narrow escape from destruction, receiving a timely warning from two boys who saw the flames.

The New York Times, New York, NY 17 Jul 1879

* * * * * * * * * * *

Just 4 years earlier, President Abraham Lincoln was shot to death by John Wilkes Booth while at the Ford Theater to see the play "Our American Cousin" with the First Lady. The Emancipation Proclamation, freeing the slaves had been signed in 1863, and the Civil War had come to and end in 1865, with the North winning over the South after several bloody confrontations, including the battle of Gettysburg in Pennsylvania. The nation was just beginning to recover from these events and the Industrial Revolution was in full swing.

The mid to late 1800's brought the birth of the railroad, bringing towns and cities closer together and allowing for cheaper and quicker transportation of goods, including the wonderful and clean anthracite coal of northeast Pennsylvania. It also made for a great escape route for the criminally minded, as well as easy access to towns that would otherwise be out of reach. Along with the good, came the bad. Centralia in 1869 was served by two railroad lines, the Philadelphia and Reading, and the Lehigh Valley line, but most passenger service ran to Allentown or Pottsville or north into Bloomsburg. Members of the Molly Maguires from other parts of the country found it easy to meet, picking locations that were readily accessible by rail. The prime agenda of the Maguires was fair wages and safe working conditions for all workers. Given the deplorable working conditions of the Pennsylvania miners, the young children working and dying in the mines and the deceased miners wives being forced from their company homes, there was certainly a lot that needed fixing. The only problem was the Maguires heinous method of going about "fixing" this sort of situation. They would not hesitate to cripple or murder anyone who got in their way, and they were making their way across Pennsylvania in the late 1800's.

It was a hot and humid mid-July afternoon and the mines had just shut down for the day.

The crowd grew quickly on this sweltering summer day outside the small mining hospital. Not in quite some time had the quiet town of Centralia seen such activity. As one local put it, "There isn't much to do in Centralia, and we like it just fine that way." Until the arrival of the Molly Maguires, the town enjoyed a safe place to live and raise a family with plenty of employment, albeit of low wage. The townspeople were generally content. Now this. The priest of St. Ignatius Roman Catholic Church lay inside, fighting for his life after having been beaten almost to death by the Maguires. He had been brought here as the closet hospital was in Ashland, over 7 miles away. The townspeople were demanding justice. It was just the previous year, 1868, that the town founder, Alexander Rae, had been brutally murdered in his buggy on his way back to Centralia from Mount Carmel, 4 miles distant. Now the Pinkerton's were involved. This great detective agency had placed moles in the Maguires ranks and were on the verge of proving their deeds and bringing them to justice, but it was not soon enough for Father McDermott.

Paul Wagenseller, who was visiting from Mauch Chunk on mining business yelled out, "What good are you people!" referring to the Pinkerton's and the numerous police authorities who were present. "These hoodlums ransacked Mauch Chunk and now they have migrated here! It is time to put them away for good!"

"Yeah! Just take 'em down! They don't even deserve prison!" yelled an older man in the crowd.

The noise level rose and the crowd was becoming agitated when a tall man wearing a uniform and sporting a wide brimmed hat and two six-shooters on his side, dismounted his pure white horse and approached, his long shadow created by the slowly setting sun preceding him. He paused, tied his horse to a post, observed the crowd and lifted his hat momentarily and wiped the sweat off his brow with a long, finely decorated red and white bandanna. Without saying a word the crowd became quiet and parted, allowing the man to pass. It was like Moses approaching and parting the Red Sea, and the locals had equal respect for this man. He was the town Sheriff and had come in on a platform of cleaning up crime and in particular of bringing down the Maguires. He was a tall man, tall and big, but in a buff way, well toned and powerful as a bull ox. He had already brought down several corrupt mine bosses and had gone up against a powerful U.S. Senator. His jail was always full with those who failed to heed the law, yet he was honest and just to those who were deserving. The townspeople were truly proud to have him leading in the fight for justice. He tipped his hat in gratitude, and disappeared into the building.

Once inside he was directed by a nurse to the bedside of the priest.

"He just woke up Sheriff and should be able to speak to you," the nurse said quietly. "Just keep it short, he needs his rest."

In the bed before him lay Father Daniel Ignatius McDermott, battered and beaten, his bloodshot eyes just beginning to re-acclimate to the light. His right leg was bound with two old rotted boards, and his chest was wrapped tight with a bed sheet. The Sheriff knelt beside him and took him by the hand.

"Father, do you know what happened to you?" said the Sheriff.

Father McDermott was silent for a moment and then began, "They came at us from behind. I was walking with Jacob McClure, who was going to do some work on the church. I don't know why they would come at us. I told Jacob to run and get help, and he must have gone after you. Next thing I know, I am lying in this bed. Sheriff, do you have any idea who came after us?"

The Sheriff too, was puzzled as to why a priest and a common worker would be targeted by the high profile Maguires, but then Father McDermott was known to badmouth the Maquires heinous methods of achieving their goals. "Father," he began. "It was three of the Maguires, Patrick Hester, Patrick Tulley and Peter McHugh. Do you have any idea why the Maguires would want to target you or perhaps the church?"

"I haven't a clue, I never spoke well of them, but neither did I threaten them," said the priest, "but I assure you as God is my witness that God will see that justice is done. They will find their place in Hell where they belong!"

The Sheriff replied, "I will help in that cause, and if you can think of anything else that could help us bring them to justice, you be sure and call for me. I will leave you now so you can rest."

"God bless you and yours, in the name of the Father, the Son and the Holy Spirit," replied the priest as he weakly made the sign of the cross and drifted into a peaceful slumber.

Summer turned to fall, and Father McDermott regained his health, still feeling the pain of mending bone and flesh, and angry at God for having forsaken him and his town. He had not preached a sermon since the incident, and Father Paul Baker had been sent in from Reading to cover his duties. Now it was time to regain his pulpit and his parishioners. He was to return to duty Sunday, November 7, 1869. He spent his 4 months in bed deciding how to approach the unfortunate situation that had befallen him. The Pinkerton's were hot on the trail of the Maguires, who would eventually be caught and would be brought to justice in 1877. They would be hanged for their murderous spree. This was of no consolation, however, to the priest, as they were still on the run with no capture in sight.

November 7 came quickly, and turned out to be a wonderfully warm and breezy day, with temperatures showing a balmy 52 degrees on the mercury thermometer in the barbershop window. A large crowd turned out for the days Mass to welcome back Father McDermott. Many not of the Catholic faith turned out as well. There was a full house as Father McDermott began. "Thank you one and all for coming out today, and may God bless you all in the name of the Father, the Son and the Holy Spirit, through him, and with him, and in him, O God, almighty Father, in the unity of the Holy Spirit, all glory and honor is yours, forever and ever. Amen." A resounding "Amen" arose from the crowd. The priest continued, "Today's Mass will be in English only and will end with a special sermon, so please remain seated at the conclusion of the regular Mass."

A Mass of mixed English and Latin was common in those days as the Mass was intended for education as much as religion. Sermons following Mass, however, were usually relegated to special events and memorials. The parishioners were not certain what to expect.

The Mass ended as usual, and upon completion the priest paused and then began, "The wrath of God has come upon me and upon this town. Unspeakable evil has come to this town, seeking their God of Gold, blaspheming not one, but all ten of God's Holy commandments, and perjuring the very spirit of the Lord. Now shall God intervene, His divine servants shall come forth upon this very earth and Damn this town and all it's vagrants into submission as it is God's will, just as it was in the story of Sodom and Gomorrah! The blessed of the town shall live their lives in Grace, but the future of this town has already been determined by the ever growing presence of evil doers and greedy earth robbing industrialists! God shall come forth and rend this town barren of coal; prosperity shall dwindle. For what has been done in this town the Lord God shall act with great hostility against us. He shall bring upon us a sword which will execute vengeance for the Covenant. He shall lay waste to this town all its people and make the land desolate such that no one shall be able to ever settle it again! The evil-doers shall fall with a sudden terror, shall be overcome by consumption and fever that shall waste away the eyes and cause the soul to pine away. They shall be served justice by Him and shall live for eternity with the beasts of Hell, being forever hungry, but never fed, and when fed, never satisfied. They shall thirst with a mouth dried by the fires of Hell and a thirst that is never quenched. And as for this town? This town shall dry up of coal and the farms shall be blighted and all living things shall die and the town shall dwindle, bit by bit until none remains but this very church, St. Ignatius Roman Catholic!" He paused and then ended with, "May God save our souls."

The protracted silence that followed was unnerving. Parishioners remained in their seats, fixated on the pulpit as the priest snuffed the candles and walked off stage left. They sat for a minute or two longer, fully expecting the priest to return to the pulpit to explain all of this, but he never came out. Quietly, in almost utter silence, the congregation left the church and returned home.

The matter was never discussed further, and only had a small byline in the Shamoken Herald, on page two no less. Yet the words of the priest were not forgotten and remain as legend until this very day.

The old man leaned back, re-lit his pipe and quietly looked upon the cracked and derelict highway before him. A spotted butterfly landed upon his shoulder and he gently transferred it to a crooked and callused finger on his left hand. He smiled and then set it free. "Not much left to smile at around here anymore," he reflected. "After the priest cursed the town the coal really did begin drying up around here. Sometimes quite unexpectedly – the anthracite seemed to just vanish. Veins that should have gone on just ended and boreholes loaded with coal when dug revealed no coal to be found. Then there was the big fire of July 17, 1879 at the Provost Mine – that one damn near took out the town! If it had caught the workings of the Continental and Hazel Dell Mines, which were only divided from the burning vein by a pillar of coal 30 feet thick, it would of burned the whole town down for sure! As I recall the New York Times reported that 'just before the fire commenced a car-load of miners, who were descending into the pit, made a narrow escape from destruction, receiving a timely warning from two boys who saw the flames.'"

The old man repositioned himself on the rock and continued. "By about 1900 the townspeople were beginning to wonder if there really was a curse upon the town. The mine owners didn't seem to think this was funny at all – they insisted their quotas be met curse or no curse. The geologists said there was coal, well the miners better dig it out! That's when one spring day in 1915 one miner took it upon himself to try and counteract the curse of the priest with one of his own, and brought in one of the most evil men to ever inhabit this earth to do the job."

His pipe failed to remain lit and he tapped it maddeningly on the stone. The remaining embers would not come out of the bowl. He reached into his pocket and pulled out what looked like a miniature toolkit contained within a small black pouch. From the pouch he retrieved a small metal tool and a short pipe cleaner. He judiciously disassembled the pipe and began working on cleaning out the tobacco remnants and residue. "You know, I've had this very pipe since 1959. A fellow miner gave it to me one day for saving his life in a mine collapse. He's dead now. Old age I suppose, God rest his soul. Since he gave it to me I only smoke it on the weekends, must be a carryover from when my wife, Jenna, was alive. She died of cancer a number of years back, God rest her soul too. Sweetest apple on the tree, but she sure couldn't stand the smell of my pipe. I tried Cherry tobacco and all sorts of other flavors, but she wouldn't have it, so on the weekends I'd go off to town and have a few beers in one of the many saloons in town. I'd meet up with the other miners and talk about politics, religion or just about anything other than mining. Guess I kind of kept up that weekend tradition in heartfelt memory of my most dearest Jenna."

A tear rolled from his left eye and his mouth quivered. He wiped his eye with the ragged white handkerchief that was stowed in his vest pocket. "I sure do miss her," he said, quietly putting his pipe back together.

"Anyway, this one mine boss had his job on the line and was determined to get his quota out of the mine regardless of any priestly curse. And it worked. For a time." He placed the unlit pipe between his teeth as if certifying it was assembled correctly, then removed it from his lips and held it lovingly in his hand.

The sky began clouding up as the old man continued his story. Evil dirty black clouds began gathering low overhead, as if a warning for us to leave and never come back. The wind picked up and the trees groaned in defiance. Black crows flew back and forth overhead. We ignored the warnings and repositioned ourselves on the ground beside the old man. His story was just beginning.

Chapter 4 – Evil Reprieve, Part 1

At a coal mine in Centralia, PA
Spring 1915

1915 was a landmark year for the United States and for the World. The war to end all wars was in progress, the U.S. had not yet got involved. In January the Rocky Mountain National Park was established by an act of Congress. The U.S. House of Representatives rejected a proposal to give women the right to vote. And in Washington DC the first stones were laid, beginning the construction of the Lincoln Memorial. But the most important thing in Centralia was getting the coal out of the ground. National and worldwide affairs affected rural America very little. Communications and transportation were slow and news did not travel fast. Besides, what difference does an overseas war, a national monument or the stock market mean to a town living hand to mouth, with a local economy not affected by such events? Only "The Maverick," Woodrow Wilson, could spoil the day for them, with his implementation of an income tax and the Federal Reserve System that would totally take charge of the U.S. currency and dominate the nation's economy, but it would take a number of years to realize the fallout of these events. In Centralia, however, coal was king, and with many of our nations men overseas preparing for battle the work of those remaining doubled.

"Move it! Move it!" shouted the gruff looking mine operator. "The boss expects 40 tons by day's end and we're 'gonna give it to him! Our jobs depend on it!"

A Loader came out of the mine entrance, covered in black coal dust. "Ain't 'gonna move no more coal until we blast boss. It's dry as a bone down there. The Overman wants you down in the hole to have a look at the situation."

Buddy, as he was called, had been operator of this mine for over 10 years. He never figured on it ever running out of coal as this mine was located on one of the richest anthracite deposits in Pennsylvania, but it was not looking good. It seems the coal veins started drying up ever since that ornery old preacher cursed the town, way back in 1869. The mine owners were threatening to relieve Buddy if he could not pull his quota from the mine and replace him with a fellow from Allentown who was moving to the area. Determined to meet his quota, Buddy proceeded down the shaft with the manager and several miners. They stopped by the lamp cabin, and grabbed some lamps and extra carbide. Buddy figured they may be down there a while. The trip down to the 700 foot level took almost half an hour. When they reached the end of the tunnel, Jim, the Overman was waiting. Not much ever fazes Jim, and at 6 foot 3, 230 pounds, few disagreed with him, and rightly so as he was rarely ever wrong.

"Boss, you have to see this," Jim started. "Geologically there should be coal here. Visually there WAS coal here. There is no way this vein should have ended. We need to blast and see what is beyond this rock. There has to be more coal."

Buddy remained silent, fixated on the solid rock wall before them, barren of coal, where coal should be. How could they have been so wrong? Does it really have something to do with the preachers curse? It seems a lot of mines have been failing since the preacher cursed the town. No, Buddy thought, this can't be.

"Let's work on the south tunnel for now," Buddy said, hoping to defer the inevitable. "I'll call down to Philadelphia for a geologist to do a survey. No point in blasting if we don't have a clue what we are going to find."

The manager agreed, and the group slowly made their way back to the surface after taking some notes for the geologist. The group was ominously quiet and went their own ways upon reaching the surface. The sun was cresting over the distant mountain and the days work was done. They were just short of quota, but Buddy figured they should be able to make it up the next day with coal from the south tunnel. They would need more wood to shore up the shaft as they were going to need to rob some of the coal to meet their quota. This was always incredibly dangerous as it weakens the mine shaft and could lead to collapse.

The mine manager slapped Buddy on the back. "Let's call it a day, better day tomorrow," he said, as he headed back to his waiting carriage.

Buddy hiked back to his small cabin near the mine. He lived in a small single home – far better than most of the miners lived in. He had been with the mining company for many years and had earned a place of his own. It was small, but pleasant – a temporary "gift" of the mining company; a warm and cozy retreat from the coal mine, and a place to wash up and sleep and to call home. When he arrived home his wife Dorothy was waiting. She had a wonderful supper prepared. Buddy cleaned his shoes on the straw mat outside and entered, each wide, weathered, gray colored board on the floor groaned as he trod on it. The warm heat from the coal cook stove took the chill off the brisk spring air. A nor'easter was blowing in and the temperatures were dropping quickly. There was going to be rough weather tomorrow.

Dorothy was a strapping woman, almost 6 feet tall and well matched to her husband. She was quite able to take care of herself, and with an occasional influx of cash sent by her mother from Philadelphia was able to provide a little extra for her husband and also was able to take an occasional trip and pretend to be wealthy. Some day she would inherit the wealth of her parents, but today was not that day. She had traveled to Europe on several occasions and to many places in the United States. She was barren from birth, but this did not bother Buddy, he knowing that she would always be able to return to her parents should something happen to him at the mine. She was also quite educated, having a proper high school degree and having spent several years at Bryn Mawr College, dropping out before graduating to travel and learn more about the local region. It was during this time in 1905 that she stumbled upon the coal region, and met Buddy. It was love at first site. Her father, a Philadelphia banker, was not pleased with her "hanging around with a poor redneck bum" and told her she could do as she pleased, but she would be on her own, cut off from the family finances. Her mother was more sympathetic to her true love, and would pass along an occasional stipend as an act of kindness.

Dorothy handed Buddy a copy of the local newspaper. Oh great, he thought, Woodrow Wilson is at it again. Great plans to change the country, great plans can only mean that the little guy will suffer. Centralize the banking, banks prosper, take the taxes away from the corporations, the people get taxed. War across the world that we may get involved in and on top of all these national and worldwide problems that are sure to hit home, the coal mine has stopped producing. Concerned about the "missing coal" and of his job at the mine, Buddy related the events of the day to his wife. He was not quite certain how to begin, knowing that whatever he said would cause her to worry over their security, little as it is working at a mine.

He began, "The north shaft ran dry, and the mine owners are still demanding we meet quota. They are threatening to replace me if our output drops, like that is going to do any good. I swear it is the preachers curse – our bore holes showed the vein going on for miles, yet we hit solid rock just yesterday. It is like Satan himself came down and dragged out all the coal!" Buddy paused. "You know, if I could go back in time I'd 'off' the Maguires myself so that they could never have attacked that ornery, vindictive old preacher!"

Dorothy set down a steaming bowl of mashed potatoes on the small maple dining table, which was just big enough for the two to dine at, but appeared much larger given the small size of the room.

"You know," she said, "God wouldn't like to hear you speak that way! Anyway, you can't go back and change time."

She trundled over to the cook stove, opened the grate, fed in a few more pieces of coal, and jostled the coals with the slicer to bring life back to the fire, hoping to speed up the teapot which was refusing to boil. She looked thoughtfully at Buddy.

"You know," she began, "maybe there is some degree of truth in that old tale."

Dorothy was well learned and had been assisting the head teacher in the local grade school. She had access to many books, and always read the old mining stories, of which many volumes were available. She had made a trip a few years back to Lansford to speak with a former mine operator who worked for the Lehigh and Wilkes Barre Coal and Navigation Company, and he had supplied at no cost a crate full of mining records and historical books and documents for the school. She had read most of them, and was particularly interested in the mine fire of 1884. All but one person, Thomas Powell, had managed to escape. He finally made it out and wrote a lengthy and very interesting report on the incident. This was one of the documents now in the possession of the grade school. She had also read the personal memoirs of a parishioner of the St. Ignatius Roman Catholic Church, who described that day in 1869 when the preacher cursed the town of Centralia for the evil that befell it. He said after the sermon the sky turned dark, and the roof and walls of the church groaned in anguish. The statue of Mary shifted from its stand and fell over, rolling almost to the pulpit. It rained a full seven days afterward, the skies being coal-black and the winds tearing branches from the trees.

She continued, "You know, we could fight fire with fire."

"How is that?" Buddy queried.

"I could get in touch with Rose Kelley in New York," she said. "She is married to Aleister Crowley – I think we could have them gather some folks who could work up a spell to counteract the preachers curse."

Aleister Crowley was heavily involved in wicked rites and had founded the magazine "Equinox" which was published from 1909 to 1913. Crowley was involved with the Golden Dawn and other "unholy" organizations, and had become known as "the Wickedest Man in the World". Crowley had married his assistant, Rose Kelley, in 1903, and Dorothy had the pleasure of meeting them on one of her travels. Always one to acquire more knowledge, Dorothy asked about their beliefs and practices, having seen a copy of the Equinox magazine. Rose was impressed, as most people she met were deathly afraid of them, and would see them hanged for their beliefs. Before parting, Rose gave Dorothy a box full of Equinox magazines and her address and contact information. They were staying in New York and were not traveling of late due to the escalating tensions in Europe, which would come to be known as "the Great War".

Dorothy placed a small roasted goose on the table, and poured water from the now steaming teapot into two small cups. She dropped in some dried dandelion roots to make a sort of ersatz coffee, and sat down with her husband at the table. "Just what if we could reverse that curse and bring back the coal. We surely could save your job, and the jobs of the 500 or so miners and our town."

"Oh poppycock!" Buddy retorted. "We don't even know if it really is a curse, or just a stroke of bad luck. I admit it seems like we're cursed, but that is a really farfetched idea."

"Well, it certainly wouldn't hurt to at least get in touch with Rose and see what she thinks. I'll wire her in the morning and tell her what is going on. In the meantime, see if you can keep up the quota at the mine and keep your job. Maybe you'll get lucky and find where all that coal went," she concluded.

Having finished their evening supper, Dorothy gathered up the plates and utensils and piled them on the stand next to the wash basin. She closed the grate on the coal stove to bring down the heat and keep the coals going longer. Then she got the box Rose had given her, sat in her small cushioned chair and pored over each piece, hoping to learn more about the infamous Aleister Crowley, and about the occult in general. Crowley, she learned, was neither a religious person nor a Satanist. In fact, he had a new sort of belief, and hoped to create a spiritual tradition that would replace all others. He was considered the most abominable human on earth by fundamentalist Christians. He attended Trinity

College in Cambridge, Massachusetts in 1895, and shortly after was vested in the trust fund given to him by his father. With his newly acquired wealth he mingled with high society. He was strongly influenced by "The Book of Black Magic and Pacts" written by Arthur Waite. He also wrote erotic and pornographic poetry. Crowley was initiated into the Golden Dawn on November 18, 1899, taking the name Frater Perdurabo, translated from the Latin to mean roughly "I will endure". Crowley defined a magician as one who can master science and art and cause change to occur at will. Magic is self understanding and the ability to put one's knowledge to practical use. He moved to New York in early 1915 after having been in Germany in 1912 (where he met Dorothy) and later in Moscow, where he promoted a dance troupe. He would spend the time from 1915 through 1919 in New York writing anti-British propaganda.

Buddy had long been in bed, and the oil in the lamp was dwindling. Dorothy packed all the documents into the stained and splintered old wooden box, lay it back in the corner next to the cupboard, snuffed the lamp, and retired for the evening.

The next two weeks would be taxing at the mine, trying to meet quota and using ever more dangerous operations around the workings in an attempt to pull all the available anthracite from the tailings and remaining workable mine shafts.

March was coming to an end, and Dorothy received a wire from Rose that she and Aleister would be arriving by train in Pottsville and then on to Mount Carmel. From Mount Carmel they would proceed on to Centralia by coach. There were other quicker routes, but Aleister had plans to visit some acquaintances and this seemed the most logical route. She said the priest's curse intrigued Aleister and he wanted to learn more, though he would make no commitment, as Aleister only commits to that which intrigues him or can benefit him personally. They were planning to arrive on Thursday, April the first, a very fitting day for this occasion. Dorothy spent days tidying their small home. The Crowley's would be staying at the Montana Hotel in town but Dorothy wanted to invite them to their home to look over the documents and discus the issues with the mine. Dorothy made a list of all the local shops for them, as Rose loved to shop at small town artisan stores, always looking for some unique local oddity to add to her estate. Dorothy knew the hotel proprietor, George Billman, personally and met with him to advise him of the visit by the strange out of town folks. George assured Dorothy that they would get the best suite in the hotel and he would personally ascertain that their stay was pleasant.

The time passed quickly, and finally April first had arrived. Buddy was working at the mine and was arranging for Crowley to visit the mine.

Some at the mine were skeptical, some were concerned, but all he spoke to felt the town was somehow cursed and were willing to try anything to bring back the good times.

Dorothy met Crowley and Rose at the hotel. Crowley, with an oval, almost square face and a perpetual frown and brusque mannerism standing beside Rose, a soft spoken queen with a thin figure and a pretty but time warn complexion, certainly made for an odd couple. She sported a wide flowing dress and wore a necklace of pearls. The couple was as out of place here as a miner would be at a Manhattan ballroom. As they sat down to lunch at the hotel, all eyes were upon them. Centralia had certainly never seen such odd folk. They had that definite "not from around these parts" look.

"It was quite the expedition, getting here," Rose said, as they waited for their meal. "This place is not a bit like New York, nor any other civilized city. Seems kind of quaint and backward if I might say so, but charming in its own way." Rose was accustomed to city life. Dorothy too had come from the city and understood how Rose felt.

"Takes quite a bit of getting used to," replied Dorothy. "Definitely not for the fainthearted."

"I have told Aleister all about your priest and the curse and he is anxious to see your manuscripts. Are we able to come by this evening?" Aleister remained quiet while Rose did the talking, all the while remaining fixated on the rustic furnishings in the hotel dining room.

"I have all the documents ready and in order for you, and my husband, Buddy is looking forward to meeting you. Is 7 o'clock OK?" Dorothy figured the two would be tired from their travels and this would give them time to rest and get organized.

"7 o'clock will be fine, is that OK with you Aleister?"

A brief nod was his only acknowledgment.

Dorothy discussed the history of the area and the local merchants and gave Rose the list she had created of local artisan shops. Rose said she would be sure to visit some of them during their stay. Rose complimented the "down home" cooking, and even Aleister finally spoke, saying if his magic were powerful enough he would magically transport the hotel and all of its staff to New York, just so he could partake of the excellent cuisine on a daily basis.

The tab was paid and Aleister and Rose settled into their suite. Dorothy headed home to prepare a meal for her husband who would be coming home soon.

Dorothy prepared a light meal of left over's and served the remaining two slices of an apple pie she had made from last year's apples that she had canned. Following their meal she quickly cleaned the dishes and prepared for the arrival of their guests. She got her box of documents and some news clippings she had cut, and Buddy brought home some mining data for Aleister to review. By the data one could clearly see the dramatic decline in mine production following the curse of the priest. If the decline continued at this pace, there would be no coal left in the entire region in less than 10 years. In addition, there had been local droughts since the curse and farms in the area were in trouble.

At 7 o'clock sharp there was a rap at the door. Aleister and Rose were right on time, probably due to the accuracy of his 22 carat gold Waltham Bartlett pocket watch and his penchant for always being on time. Dorothy directed the couple to the small dining table, and turned up the wick on the oil lamp hanging above it. The four spent the next three hours going over the documents and discussing the situation. Rose, who was known as being clairvoyant, said she perceived something to be wrong from the time of her arrival. Aleister added that if the curse was put in place by a priest, it would most likely require a satanic spell to overcome it. He told them that he does not deal in such spells or beliefs, but had a group of practitioners coming to town who could possibly help. They were to arrive Friday morning and he said he would fill them in and see what they suggest. He let Buddy and Dorothy know that it is not wise to go against a Catholic priest, even when his demands are unwarranted or even evil. Really awful things can happen that can linger long into the future. He advised her that even good deeds when done out of greed, can come back threefold in vengeance. He told her he would take no responsibility for negative consequences. Buddy and Dorothy agreed to the terms. The four planned to meet again in the morning and speak with the others who would be arriving then.

The sun peaked out above the distant mountains, its warm early spring rays heating the air quite comfortably. The four met at the station just before 9am. The 9:15 am train arrived right on time. The only passengers that disembarked were 6 of the seediest looking characters one could imagine. They made even the Molly Maguires look like kittens. Each sported several days' growth of beard, ragged unkempt hair, pants threadbare and worn through and ragged felt hats that looked like the train had run them over. Each had a mean look on his face like the world was about to end and they were going to be the ones to stop it. As they got off the train dust rose from each one. Passerby made haste to avoid the group as they approached the street.

"Aleister," the tallest of them called out.

Aleister tipped his hat. "Hey Jimmy!" he replied.

"Been a long time old friend. Must be a real winner here to be calling us in." Jimmy removed his hat revealing a semi balding head, with curly brown hair showing just light touches of gray. A deep scar ran down the side of his left cheek. "You know Davey, Freddy, Mac and Big Joe. Don't think you ever had the pleasure of meeting Sledge."

"Why do they call him Sledge?" Aleister asked.

"He was in a bar in the Chinese section of Philadelphia when some big fella came up to him and told him he was sittin' in his seat. Sledge got up, made a face that would of scared a polar bear, turned around and beat the teak-wood bar with his right hand. Now that old bar was solid as the ground we're standing on, but the force of that right arm just cracked it apart into splinters. The big guy spun around and left, don't think he ever came back to that bar. The whole place cheered and the barkeep dropped a bottle of his best rum on the table with a double shot glass and said 'here ya go, sledge, it's on the house', this in reference to the sledge hammer force of his pounding. Reckon the name stood ever since."

Sledge wrinkled a smile, proud of his accomplishment.

"Jimmy, this is Dorothy, the miner's wife I was telling you about. We will be working with her and her husband Buddy"

"'Mam," replied Jimmy, tipping his filth ridden hat, the dust lifting into the air as he placed it back upon his head. "Well, what are we waitin' for? Daylight's a burnin'! Let's get over to that mine and see what's goin' on."

The group arrived at the main gate to the mine where they met Buddy. They headed over to the store and entered the small cabin like structure stocked with all the latest colliery tools and supplies required to operate the mine. The store boss, Franky, tipped his hat and left, closing the door behind him. Aleister and Buddy went over the history of the mining in the town, the curse of the priest and the unusual and sudden decline of the anthracite. They then toured the mine workings and came up with a plan to rid the town of the curse that had lingered so long. They would need torches and black cloth. Sulfur and pine needles. They would need blood as a sacrifice to the demons – animal blood from the local butcher would do just fine. And they would need several hundred pounds of fresh blasted anthracite to be burned as an offering. An altar would be made from a large block of coal.

Buddy had made sure that he was in full control of the mine operations over the weekend, and put up the six servants of Satan in an outbuilding just outside the gates of the mine. The building was used as a temporary residence when needed and had bunks, a well and an outhouse just outside. The six seemed pleased with their accommodations and planned to work through the night and into Saturday on their conjurations.

The group then parted ways and would not meet again until late Saturday night – the spell to be cast at midnight.

The wind was now angrily buffeting the trees as a light rain began falling. The old man took a break from his story and pushed some tobacco into his pipe. He struck a match and the wind carried the match off, flame and all, snuffing it in defiance. The old man grew angry at the wind and fired up three matches at once. The wind attacked the matches with a vengeance, but the old man won out against mother nature, cupping his vest over the pipe as he brought the leaves within to life. "You know, the first smoke of a new bowl is always the best," he said, "no ash to ruin the flavor. Much like the first coal from a mine, clean and easy, very little blasting required. Then you get down deep and it gets dirty and dangerous. All that choke damp and fire damp, either will choke you to death or blow you to bits. Then there's the danger of a mine collapse, sometimes all of its own accord, sometimes because you got greedy and robbed the pillars holding up the mine. Sometimes better just to leave it be. That's what the pillars are for – keep the mine from collapsing. Then sometimes them stupid bootleggers come along and rob the pillars, wonder why they get buried alive! Yep, just like old tobacco, you should just dump it and start fresh."

The rain stopped and the wind died just a bit, but the black clouds remained as guardians of an evil secret. Hundreds of black crows wafted back and forth in a frenzy and drifted with the wind.

The old man stared ahead, fixated on a chalk image of Satan painted on the pavement. "It ain't right to mess with the devil, no sir. Just ain't right. He'll always get you in the end – call in that IOU."

The winds picked up again as the old man continued.

Chapter 5 – Evil Reprieve, Part 2

Saturday, April 3, 1915

The moon shone brightly in the sky, just 3 days past full, lighting the coal mine as if sunrise was just around the corner. But it was not, it was ten o'clock at night. The troupe of ten, Buddy and Dorothy, Aleister and Rose, and the 6 bad hombres from Philadelphia, had gathered on a grassy field, just outside the main mine shaft. There was a cool spring breeze blowing in from the south. A trough of water was laid beside a bonfire made in a pit. Only the 6 would be situated around the pit performing the ceremony. The others would watch from a distance. By 11 pm cakes and ale were consumed, and a prayer was said for a successful ritual. It was midnight and the six sinister ministers of evil, each wearing long robes of black with pointed hoods and white under-dressings, lit a torch of wax and sulfur and held it high in the air. The bright flames flickered on the ground and the stench of burning sulfur drifted over the mine.

Jimmy began shoveling coal into the fire. "Hail Satan! Ruler of the universe! I command you to see this ritual through and throw back the curse that has been placed upon this land!" Smoke belched from the pit as the coal chunks came to life crackling like pork skins thrown into hot oil.

"I invoke and conjure thee, O Baphomet. I invoke and conjure thee O Belial!" continued Davey, holding a silver chalice filled with wine and embossed with satanic symbols high in the air, as Jimmy rang a large brass bell. "And, fortified with the power of the Supreme Majesty, I strongly command thee by the most potent prince's evil. I exorcise and command thee, O Spirit, by Him Who spake and it was done, by the Most Holy and glorious. Thou do forthwith appear and show thyself unto me, here before this circle, in a fair and human shape, without any deformity or horror; do thou come forthwith, from whatever part of the world, and manifest that which I desire, being conjured by the Name of the Eternal, Living and True God, I conjure thee also by the particular and true Name of thy God to whom thou owest thine obedience; by the name of the King who rules over thee, do thou come without tarrying; come, fulfill my desires; persist unto the end, according, to mine intentions."

The fire in the pit grew angry and spat chunks of burning coal and hot ash. Acrid sulfurous fumes and ugly black clouds vomited from the pit.

More coal and incense was thrown upon the fire. The moon quickly vanished behind a blanket of gray fog. Wolves howled in the distance, not daring to near the pit of evil. A thick steam of gray-black smoke arose from the pit and formed into a human like figure. Its form gyrated to and fro as if anxious to return to the pit.

"Welcome, spirit," began Freddy and Mack in unison, both lighting 13 large black candles sitting upon the altar made of coal, working from end to end and meeting at the center, invoking satanic names as each one was lit. They both lit the 13th candle in the name of the Father, the Son and the Holy Ghost. "Welcome art thou unto me; I have called through Him Who created Heaven, Earth and Hell, with all contained therein, and thou hast obeyed, also by the like power. I bind thee to remain affably and visibly before this circle, within this triangle, so long as I need thee, to depart not without my license, till thou hast truly and faithfully fulfilled all that I shall require."

The earth shuddered and cracks formed in the ground before them. Dark black clouds formed above. The winds shifted from the North, bringing cold air with them. The crickets became silent and the trees stirred not, despite the strong breeze. The wolves continued to howl in the distance and a swarm of bats fueled the fire, igniting from the heat and falling one by one into the pit.

The ritual continued on as Big Joe commanded the demons to evict the curse laid upon the land, demanding no repercussions. The dialog went from Jimmy to Davey to Freddy and Mack, and then back to Jimmy. At each command more coal and incense was added to the fire and the eerie figure of smoke writhed in pain. Following a final "so mote it be" it was Sledge's turn to close the ritual.

Sledge began in a gruff and curt tone, "O spirits, because thou hast diligently answered my demands, I do hereby license thee to depart, without injury to man or beast. Depart, I say, and be thou willing and ready to come, whensoever duly exorcised and conjured by the sacred rites of magick. I conjure thee to withdraw peaceably and quietly, and may peace continue forever between me and thee. Amen."

"So mote it be," the others responded.

There followed a long silence that lasted almost 30 minutes, the six staring intently into the fire pit as though ensuring the evil had returned whence it came. The evil being of smoke curled back into the pit and the sparks became quiet as blue flames issued from beneath the burning coal and wood. The air was filled with the odor of myrrh and frankincense and of burning coal and sulfur. Jimmy picked up the bucket of blood and passed it to Davey saying, "This blood is a gift in thanks for answering our demands." Davey passed it to Freddy saying, "This gift shall protect us in all our undertakings." Freddy passed it to Mack saying, "May God and Satan dine peaceably at the table." Mack passed it to Big Joe saying, "So mote it be!" and passed it to Sledge who picked up the large bucket and tossed the blood into the pit screaming, "I thrust aloft the bifid barb of hell and on its tines resplendently impaled my sacrifice through vengeance rests! Shemhamforash! Hail Satan!"

With a flash and a loud bang the pit of fire resounded coughing its last breath of smoke. Ash and sparks flew into the air looking like a massive display of fireworks. The blood boiled and spattered on the hot coals. A massive bolt of forked lightning came from the sky striking the lamp cabin and blasting off part of its roof. Then came another, blasting a telegraph pole into splinters. The six remained steadfast. Then came the rain and the cold wind. And it rained. And rained some more. In fact it rained a full seven days, flooding the town.

They cleaned up the area, made certain the fire had gone out, left the mine and parted ways working their way through the pouring rain. The six were on the morning train back to Philadelphia and Aleister and Rose would return to New York after Rose helped the local economy by spending some of Aleister's money on local trinkets and beeswax, as well as some local honey.

Buddy and Dorothy returned home, waiting to see what Monday would bring.

It was still raining Monday morning, though not as bad as it was over the weekend. Buddy had scheduled himself to be in late that day and arrived at the mine about noon. He arrived to cheers and handshakes. They had blasted the rock at the dead end tunnel and sure enough, the vein continued on!

"Damn," said Jim. "It's just like someone up and magically put the coal back in the ground! Maybe we did kick that preachers curse out of town!"

Buddy just grinned. It was going to be a good day. Everything was going to be alright!

The clouds were parting and the old man sat back. The harsh rays of the low sun accentuated every well earned wrinkle on his face. He held his pipe, unlit, in his hand which he rested on his knee. "Not 'gonna be all right. Not 'gonna be all right one bit. The devil always gets his due." He pulled a wrinkled hand drawn map from his pocket. "All these veins opened up for the miners. More anthracite then anyone could have imagined! For thirty plus years this town prospered. The mining was a bit slow during the Great War due to all the men being overseas in the military, but it picked up right good afterward. Only slowed a bit during the Great Depression – for us, we was so poor we really didn't feel no pain, and we really didn't need to pay much heed to the stock market. We still had our coal, and our bread, and our vittles. Anyway the mines were overflowin' with coal for the next 30 or so years, after which production slowed, but that was mainly due to less demand, with natural gas and crude oil taking over. The townspeople pretty much forgot about the old preachers curse. They all thought life was good."

The old man squinted at the sun which was going to be fading over the horizon soon. "Better get to the point, the whole purpose of me ramblin' on. We gotta get you folks back to your vehicle before the Gatekeeper comes out! You know, there always was a gatekeeper at the St. Ignatius but after the town died we thought the gatekeeper moved away. Seems he still comes, every morning at sunrise to open the gates, and again at sunset to close them. If you look real close though you can see there is something not quite right with him. Pretty much just a skull and bones. Not human – just the ghost of an old miner who keeps watch over the cemetery. If you meet up with him on your way back, just pay him no heed. If you look him strait in the eyes, your soul will be sucked in and you will take a permanent vacation in Hell!"

He peered over his shoulder, as if checking for some unseen danger.

"Anyways, sometime in 1932 the Devil came a-calling, came to collect his IOU. Fortunately a group of nuns from the convent stepped in to save the day and put the genie back in the bottle – for a time, at least."

Chapter 6 – Satan Calls His Hand

1932 – Bast Colliery, Near Centralia

"My name is Raymond J. Milius, I was born in Girardville Jan. 7th, 1924. Many a Saturday, My Father, my brother, and I, picked coal from the coal refuge bank, at the foot of the slope located across the creek from the drift, of the "Bast" colliery. About 1932 the mine caught fire, rumors were that the cause was a miner smoking, who left the butt lit. To extinguish the fire, it was to be flooded, the drift was blasted shut. The year was 1943. I visited Girardville, with three of my friends who were to be inducted into the army. Due to the energy shortage, the "Bast" drift was opened and the water was drained. The mine was still burning, the drift was closed. The mine was re-flooded in 1960 when my wife and I, on our "Honeymoon", drove to Shamokin, PA. On the north side of the highway from Mt. Carmel to Shamokin, driving at night, the westward red glow on the mountain was very visible, from the burning coal vein."

Signed; Raymond J. Milius. (Date unknown)

* * * * * * * * * *

1932 marked the 200th anniversary of George Washington's birth. Automobiles and motion pictures and radio were in their heyday. It was the year that the notorious gangster Al

Capone was sent to prison, only by way of his tax evasion. It was also the peak of the Great Depression, and although most small towns suffered less during the depression, the economy of towns that relied on their products or services being purchased outside of town fell, as those who normally would purchase from them were left without the resources to do so. This was also the year that a very dangerous mine fire started in Centralia.

It was Tuesday, December 20, 1932 when Satan came calling to collect his debt. There had been a light snowstorm the night before which left the ground glistening with about two inches of snow and ice. The temperature rose above freezing by dawn, and the day was wind free and quite comfortable. It was high noon at the Bast colliery just outside of Centralia when the westerly mine tunnel blew. It was lunchtime and the mineshaft had been cleared for an inspection. Just as two Federal mine inspectors were about to enter the mine the ground began to rumble, an ominous slow churning rumble which grew louder by the second. A huge puff of smoke belched out of that pit and a red fireball filled the sky throwing sparks, red hot coal clinkers and rocks as big as watermelons at the miners. Flames and sparks roared out of that shaft for 15 minutes, after which a huge shadowy figure of smoke appeared coming from the shaft. It gyrated to and fro and grew ever larger. One could see the outline of a figure; an evil figure. What appeared to be disembodied human members; arms and legs, a head and torso here and there; appeared in the smoke. The miners ran in fear of their lives. The mine bosses left with them and reassembled at the main gate to the mine. From a distance the mine now resembled the very pit of Hell, as though a portal had opened the gates and let out all the demons of Hell.

One old timer frantically exclaimed, "It's the preachers curse! It's the preachers curse!" and hurriedly fled the mine on foot.

The story of the preacher placing a curse on Centralia was pretty much lost to history, but remained steadfast as a legend passed down from generation to generation. Could this curse really be coming true this very day?

Sparks continued to rain from above and the mine bosses sent the workers home for the day warning them to not tell a soul what they had seen until it was sorted out.

The earth trembled again violently and several large cracks opened in the ground belching acrid smoke.

The mine operator pulled Joe Fishman, the shop foreman aside. Joe was in charge of the workshop where the mining equipment was repaired and new equipment was made ready for installation. His arms were thick and strong from years of moving heavy mining equipment around, and from performing maintenance on all manner of equipment, from the drilling and blasting equipment to the rail cars that moved the coal out of the mine. He supervised a staff of 10 full time mechanics, all level headed God fearing Christians. He himself was of the Jewish faith, kind of the odd man in the lot. He would often say that with so few of Jewish decent in town, he had to bless his own food and pray that God would forgive any transgressions. He made it on occasion to Saturday services in Wilkes Barre, there being few synagogues anywhere near Centralia. The miners respected him as it takes a strong will and a lot of personal conviction to stand by your personal beliefs when they differ from others beliefs. The mine operators too respected and trusted him.

"Joe," the mine operator began. "I have a mission for you. I need you to go over to St. Ignatius in town and speak quietly with the priest about what is going on. Maybe you could take the car and bring him back to the mine."

The boss treasured his 1930 Packard 740 Custom Eight convertible, one of the most expensive automobiles made at the time. He purchased the car from a dealer in Philadelphia and never let anyone drive it. Joe figured their situation must be truly dire for the boss to be letting him use his car.

"Sure boss – I'll take real good care of your car," Joe replied. "How much should I tell the priest?"

"Just give him enough information to persuade him to come on over, and be sure to remind him about the preachers curse!" answered the boss.

Joe got in the car admiring the beautiful giant tires with large whitewalls and ornate spoked wheels with the spare tire mounted in front of the door and a wonderfully curious rumble seat bringing up the rear. The top was up to keep out the cold, but it didn't seem to help very much, but Joe didn't care. The ride in this magnificent carriage would help him to forget the demons swarming out from below. He put the car in gear and it quietly began moving forward, its large tires absorbing all the imperfections in the road.

The beautiful bright red automobile slowly vanished into the distance.

Joe arrived at the church and was escorted to the main rectory by two nuns who so closely resembled one another they might have been twins. The Priest arrived, went before the altar and crossed himself, mumbling something in Latin. He then looked Joe up and down as if wondering why this filthy, coal covered person should require his immediate attention. "What brings you here?" the priest inquired.

"Father," Joe began "I was sent by the mine boss, I believe you know him well. We have an urgent matter that requires your assistance."

"Ah, yes. But what possibly could I do for the mine?"

Joe contemplated how to present the situation to the priest, then decided there was no time to waste, best just to belt it out. "Father, we feel there may be an evil presence from a curse that was set in motion in 1915 to counteract the 19th century curse of the priest – we feel the demons may have come to collect this debt. I know this sounds silly, and it would be much easier and make more sense if you came to see it for yourself."

"You mean you think your mine requires an exorcism?" The priest quietly snickered, silly young folk, he thought. "You know, you may be way off base here. Probably it is just something that is explainable if you look at it from a different angle. Really, demons?"

"Father, this is really something terrible and unexplainable by any known cause. It is like nothing we have ever seen before, and we've seen some winners!"

"Well, you know that an exorcism is a lengthy process requiring proof of possession. It also requires the approval of the Vatican and many special procedures. Protocol must be followed. Few are versed in such matters. It would pretty much have to be a definitive possession, and that is not something you can easily prove."

"Father," begged Joe, "please trust me, this won't wait – we really need your help if there anything you can do. At least come have a look. I think you will believe me just by seeing what is going on with your own eyes. It really won't take but a few minutes of your time. Then, if you still think there are no demons and it is just our imagination you can be on your way."

One of the nuns approached the priest and whispered in his ear. The priest went behind the altar to a small cabinet which contained several dusty old volumes. He retrieved a very old looking, yellowed parchment document, bound with some sort of twine. He spent a few minutes carefully leafing through the document. "I will come with you, me and my two best nuns who will assist me in reviewing your situation. I am not sure of what value we can be, but if what you say is true, we must do something to bring peace to your mine." The priest gathered some vials of holy water, several wooden crucifixes and some other supplies which he packed into a large cloth bag, and the four left the church.

Joe returned to the mine with the priest. He had been gone almost an hour. It was now 3 pm. The priest brought along the two nuns, who had assisted in cleansing a house which was presumed haunted in Shamokin some years ago. Whether it was really haunted and the nuns actually cleansed it is up for debate, but they were definitely fearless and willing to consider the unknown. The priest and two nuns came out of the car, the nuns being dwarfed by the 6 foot 5 inch frame of the priest. They walked over to the mine boss, who explained what had happened and allowed then a better view through his field glasses.

The priest was shocked at what he saw. The priest had never seen or heard of anything like this. He shook off his fear and laid a plan to send the demons back to Hell and then seal the mine. Joe was to bring in his men and equipment and stand at the ready to seal the mine once the demons retreated.

"Are you certain this will work," asked the mine boss.

"Not a clue," answered the priest, "but it is the best we have at this point. God's will be done, not ours, we can only ask and pray. If we perform this service for you, you are to tell no one. We are going out of our scope and without the OK of the Vatican, and there are no guarantees that anything we attempt will even work. I recommend keeping present only those you trust to keep our secret."

Joe sent away all of the unnecessary staff and then assembled the remaining men and equipment and loaded his trucks with clay and cement. They stood at the ready, field glasses in hand, and would await a sign from the priest before moving in to seal the mine.

The priest and both nuns moved with confidence toward the pit, all the while praying in Latin. The priest was throwing holy water ahead of him as he walked, and the nuns were waiving censers burning Myrrh and Frankincense. The pit belched smoke and fire at them and groaned in defiance. More demons appeared. It seemed that Satan was determined to reclaim the land as promised.

"In nomine Patris et Filii et Spiritus Sancti!" began the priest. "Be gone and forever return to the depths of Hell!"

Lightning bolts flashed all around the pit, emanating from the pit itself and from the soot and ash agitating the air. A hot ember landed on the priests robe, charring it. He casually flicked it off, trying to avoid showing fear.

He continued, "God, the Father of mercies, through the death and resurrection of his Son has reconciled the world to himself and sent the Holy Spirit among us for the forgiveness of sins; through the ministry of the Church, return whence you came and be forever gone." He threw more holy water at the pit. Hot clinkers spit out from the pit, just missing the priest. "Lift up your heads, O gates; And be lifted up, O ancient doors; That the King of glory may come in!; Who is the King of glory?, The Lord strong and mighty; The Lord mighty in battle; Lift up your heads, O gates; And lift them up O ancient doors; That the King of glory may come in!; Who is the King of glory?; The Lord of hosts, He is the King of glory!"

The pit belched smoke and fire and each flame was a demon, as was each waft of smoke. The pit roared and belched choking fumes of sulfur. Hot ash and embers rained down from above, having been spit from the pit. Through the roar could be vaguely heard a hissing, groaning sound, "This town shall be mine! Your God can not save you preacher!"

The priest was pushed to the ground by a hot blast of steam and smoke. The nuns lifted him from the ground and he continued. "You have no command over God! God has the power over you! You are weak, thrown from Heaven by the King of Kings. You shall burn forever deep in the bowls of Hell. Back! Back from whence you came! I order you in the name of the Father, the Son and the Holy Spirit!"

Evil eyes stared from three bright flames. A forked tongue of fire reached from the center of the pit and burned the priest. "Where is your God now?" could be heard coming from the pit, the voice modulated on the loud roar of the fire.

The priest held his large crucifix high. "The Lord of hosts is with us! The God of Jacob is our stronghold! Come; behold the works of the Lord, who has wrought desolation's in the earth. He breaks the bow and cuts the spear in two; he burns the chariots with fire!"

A huge dead tree was uprooted by a blast from the ground and headed, flaming, toward the priest.

The priest dodged the tree and continued, unabated, "He shall be exalted among the nations; he shall be exalted in the earth! The lord of hosts is with us; the God of Jacob is our stronghold!"

The priest ran close to the pit and threw the wooden crucifix into it. There came from the pit a huge blast of smoke and steam, throwing the priest and the two nuns to the ground. Clouds of dust arose from where they fell, and they fell so hard that the earth was indented where they landed. As fast as the blast ascended it withdrew back into the pit. Muted groans of agony came from the pit.

Slowly the smoke and fire began retreating into the pit as well. The priest and nuns continued for almost an hour, reciting prayers alternating with the chanting of hymns, concluding with a slow and emotional recitation of the Lord's Prayer, first in English, then in Latin.

The priest motioned to Joe to seal the pit. Joe moved his crew in and began dumping many tons of rock, clay and cement into the fissures and finally into the steaming pit, the demons having been beaten down by the priest. The whole operation lasted just over 5 hours, and by the time they were done it was as if nothing happened that fateful day. Those present were sworn to secrecy, and by virtue of the nature of the incident, none would venture to relate the story for fear of disbelief and that their sanity might be questioned.

The old man yawned and stretched, setting his pipe upon the rock beside him. "So the story goes. But legend has it that the mine fire never was contained and burns to this day. Some say it kindled the mine fire in 1962 that destroyed our town. Few wanted to believe it was demons that caused this fire, demons that were lurking underground, ever working to escape. That disbelief would spell our eventual downfall. Carelessness would cause the gates to open once again and ultimately cause the destruction of this town."

He fiddled with his pipe for a moment, re-filled it and fired it up again. Beautiful rings of smoke drifted upward, wrapping themselves around the old man's head before drifting off into space.

"A lot of folks blame the mine owners too. Round about 1951 the town petitioned for the mineral rights to the ground beneath the town. This was made possible by a new Pennsylvania law enacted a couple of years earlier. They were granted the rights. The mine owners weren't too happy though, with tens of millions of dollars worth of anthracite sitting just below the city. The only way to get to that coal would be to demolish the town and strip mine. By the 1960's most of the mining had stopped, save for a few bootleggers and strip mine operations. Seemed the only way the miners cold gain eminent domain would be if all the townspeople were to vacate the town. Seems an underground fire that could not be controlled would be the perfect way to get control of the town, and the coal. With no residents, the town could be declared vacated and could be taken over by the state, which could then turn the rights over to the mine companies, for a fee, of course. Lots of money to be made by all parties; except for the town itself. It was the fire of 1962 that got the townspeople thinking that this might just have been the plan. In fact, the town was condemned and all but seven properties and a dozen or so folks remain today. Oddly, they have been granted permission to stay for the remainder of their lives, perhaps to guard the pit and keep the demons from escaping? Well, I am getting ahead of myself here."

The old man paused and blew a few more rings of smoke. A light fog blew in from the east as the warmth of the sun began to dwindle.

"Anyway, all the problems began May 7, 1962, at the borough council meeting with a plan to clean up the landfill that had just recently been set up around the corner from the Odd Fellows cemetery to replace the one that had to be closed by the St. Ignatius cemetery. Folks would be coming to the cemetery to visit loved ones and departed veterans, and to celebrate their service to our nation on Memorial Day. Who could possibly object to cleaning up the landfill? Well, problem was, most small towns, including Centralia, used fire to rid their town of waste, even though this is not generally sanctioned by the state."

The old man pondered for a moment, and blew a few more rings for us. The air was ominous with the light fog and the slowly setting sun. We would be walking back in the dark, but the story was too far along for us to leave now, with the tale unfinished.

"As you shall see, it was this very fire that spread and opened the old mine pit, releasing the demons once again and setting the coal vein on fire causing the eventual loss of our great town. But first, if I may digress, a bit of the interim history is required to understand what happened prior to Memorial Day, 1962."

Chapter 7 – Centralia, PA

1935 through 1962

Much of the history of Centralia between 1935 and 1962 has been lost to time. Many of the borough records of this time period no longer exist. There were no computers to store data, and small town history (aside from births, deaths and elections, which also got recorded in state records) was considered transient and inconsequential. Some information can be found in period newspapers – if you can find them. Again, nothing was ever saved for future reference. By way of background, a few local, national and global events that occurred during this time should be understood.

Coal led the pack as a source of energy from the late 1800's through about 1950. During this time coal used for stoves, for steam powered locomotives and for the generation of electricity was in its prime. As time passed, oil and gasoline, and then natural gas, took over many of these functions. Steam powered trains were gradually phased out and coal for heating and cooking became a holdout only in the most rural areas, where many still use coal to this very day. This was also the time of mass urbanization. Coal and big cities don't go together well, as the smog years of London, England, proved.

Coal usage declined during the Great Depression, and many mines closed, including 5 in Centralia.

Then, World War II came. With a vast majority of young men off fighting the war in Europe, few remained behind to work in the mines. Iron and steel ruled, much of it recycled, and women came into the workforce. The mines rarely employed women due to the extreme conditions in the mines.

After the war ended coal never rebounded. The Interstate Highway system was evaluated by FDR in 1941 and implementation was begun in 1952, first as tolled segments, later as either tolled or federally funded non-tolled roads. President Eisenhower worked out a funding plan for the United States highway system (which was begun in 1952 but did not reach official completion until 1991.) Gasoline and diesel began moving people and goods. Steam trains were replaced with cleaner and more efficient diesel engines as well.

1949 saw the enactment of a very interesting law in Pennsylvania – a law which allowed municipalities to purchase the mineral rights for their town. Little is written about this, but it is interesting to note that only one town, Centralia, chose to exercise this option. The rights were handed over by the mining companies, who weren't mining anyway at the time, to the town.

As time passed, it became evident that a great majority of the anthracite coal lay beneath the town of Centralia. In the late 1950's there was a resurgence of coal fired electrical generation plants, which burn a lot of anthracite coal. The coal companies began scrambling for sources of the clean burning anthracite needed to run these plants. In many of those towns that had not elected to purchase the mineral rights the residents were evicted by the mine owners and the towns were leveled and strip mined. The mine owners could not touch Centralia, however, as the town owned the underground mineral rights, and this is one of the reasons that some people believe there was a conspiracy to let the 1962 mine fire burn. By law, if the state could declare the town uninhabitable and take it over by eminent domain, it would acquire the mineral rights by default, and could sell those rights to the mining companies.

By 1962 virtually all mining in Centralia had ceased, and the town was in decline, but was still fully functional, with the residents going about their business as usual.

Chapter 8 – Council Meeting

Centralia Town Hall, May 7, 1962

The year was 1962. John Fitzgerald Kennedy, the 35th and youngest U.S. President, was in the second year of his short Presidency, and was dealing with the Cuban missile crisis, one of the toughest situations in American history, as well as tensions in Vietnam. The Beatles failed to cut the muster with record label Decca, but would remain steadfast in their determination on signing a record label. It was also the year that the Navy Seals were established. In Centralia, 1962 marked the beginning of a slow and painful death. Coal usage peaked in the early 1900's. Centralia lost five mines owned by the Lehigh Valley Coal Company in 1929 due to the stock market crash and economic situation. Oil and Gas became King and Queen beginning in the 1950's, leaving coal behind in the dust. By 1962 almost all coal production in Centralia had ceased, save a couple of strip mines and the independent and daring "pillar robbers", who would remove and sell the coal pillars that the mine companies had left to support the mine shafts. The town of Centralia was already in serious decline when the mine caught fire leading to the eventual demise of the town.

May was an important month in Centralia. The big highlight was always Memorial Day, with its wonderful celebrations in remembrance of those who fought and died to keep our country free. It was one of the few days that the entire town banded together in harmony. Most non-essential workers were given the day off from work; a rare treat indeed. It was a time to show off the town, to clean it up for the celebration, to be proud of the town. Thus, the main topic of the May council meeting was always getting all the parade permits in order, and of course, the town cleanup in preparation for the holiday.

Monday, May 7, 1962 was a cool day, with a high temperature of only 61 degrees. Mayor George Winnick and the 7 Centralia borough council members took their seats at the regular council meeting. There would be plenty to discuss at this meeting, and it was this meeting that set in place the events leading to the ultimate loss of this quaint, once productive, rural mining town.

The business went on as usual, with the major topic being Memorial Day, which was Wednesday, May 30. Many events were planned and all required approval of the council.

The most urgent topic was held for last. That was the cleanup of the town dump, which had been adjacent to the St. Ignatius Roman

Catholic Church cemetery, and which had been moved in early 1962 to the old Edward Whitney strip mine which was abandoned in 1935 and which was located adjacent the northeast corner of the Odd Fellows Cemetery. This site was chosen because it was being used as an "informal dump" already, and being 300 feet long 75 feet wide and 50 feet deep would provide a good long term disposal solution. It also had good road access. Councilman Joseph Tighe, who was in charge of all landfill matters, had negotiated a lease with the Lehigh Valley Coal Company, which owned the pit, and obtained their blessing to use it for a landfill. George Segaritus, regional landfill inspector for the state Department of Mines and Minerals Industries (DMMI), approved of the site but was concerned about several holes in the walls and floor of the pit. Strip mines in Pennsylvania often cut through old mine shafts, and this mine was no exception. He advised Tighe that all these holes would need to be filled with non-combustible material so that should a fire start it would not be able to spread to adjacent mines. Tighe received council approval and had all the holes sealed and inspected.

Councilman John May addressed the council and reminded them that Memorial Day was approaching and suggested that council clean up the new Centralia landfill. Being so near the cemetery it needed to look tidy since the Memorial Day festivities took place at the cemetery nearby and in view of the landfill. Every year members of the American Legion in Centralia would form a color guard and march behind it from cemetery to cemetery, firing volleys to honor the dead. Families and friends went to the cemeteries to honor the deceased Veterans and tend their graves.

The landfill cleanup was unanimously approved, after all, who could object to cleaning up the town in preparation for one of the more important holidays?

The method for cleaning up the landfill was not discussed and can only be deduced from town records and word of mouth. In general, the landfill was set on fire; the fire was allowed to consume the rubbish and was then put out by the local fire department. This was never made a part of council discussion or minutes as such methods are not permitted by Pennsylvania law. This is however, how most small towns have done this, as it is the most cost effective way to reduce the amount of rubbish and eliminate rats, other vermin and odors.

While the method for cleaning the landfill was not discussed at the council meeting, the date was – it was to be Monday, May 27, two days prior to Memorial Day.

When asked by the press how the cleanup was to be done, the council President replied "In the usual manner," meaning that public works would be in charge of the operation and would be permitted to determine the best method for the cleanup. Enough said. Everyone pretty much knew how it was done, and that no public record should exist due to the nature of the operation.

The council meeting adjourned and all departed into the chilly 46 degree early May evening.

The following week the Public Works department met with local Fire Chief James Cleary, Jr. and his Assistant Chief, Thomas Krupinski and planned the cleanup. Public Works officials would tidy up the rubbish pile with heavy equipment and then would set the pile ablaze. The fire fighters were to be paid to put out the fire once the rubbish was consumed. Again, none of this is official public record, but there are on file receipts for services rendered that prove this occurred. In any event, how it happened is not relevant to this story, the fact is there was a fire in the landfill May 27 and it was put out by a group of local fire fighters. Or so they thought.

Chapter 9 – Landfill Cleanup

Town Landfill, Sunday, May 27, 1962

"Hey Mac," yelled the driver in the cab of the large yellow bulldozer. "Clear the people from the area around the landfill – I'm going to start moving the stuff on the outer perimeter to the center."

Mac nodded and proceeded to move him and the other workers from the area. Mac had been in charge of landfill cleanup operations for as long as anyone could remember, and was good at what he did and was well respected.

It was going to be a nice day, partly cloudy and highs only in the low 70's. A perfect day to burn down the rubbish in the landfill. This operation was always kept quiet and "off the books" since while it was a common practice in a small town to burn down the landfill, it was a practice not sanctioned by the state.

Several members of the Centralia Fire Department would be arriving soon to oversee the operation and to put out the fire once the rubbish had burned down, an operation that was routine for them, as this had been done this way for many years. It has been said that in Centralia "there was a burn at the landfill practically every weekend" and there was usually a larger burn when the landfill was cleaned up in preparation for a major holiday.

A half dozen fire fighters and two fire trucks arrived at the landfill just before noon and got out to survey the area. The Chief and Assistant Chief were present, as were a few trusted old-timers. They also brought with them a young scrawny green rookie just learning the ropes. One of their regular crew was unable to make it and they figured the rookie should be able to handle something as simple as a trash fire. More concerning was whether this rookie would be able to keep the operation quiet. This would prove a good test of loyalty and a good learning experience for the rookie. They began setting up their equipment and hose lines. When they were satisfied that all was OK the order was given to "light it up". The bulldozer driver jumped down and dumped some kerosene on the pile and set it ablaze.

The group of municipal workers and fire fighters then gathered to admire their work. The burn down would take five or six hours, and the process had to be watched the entire time. Mac drove off in his pickup truck and returned within an hour's time with his truck bed loaded with sandwiches and cold drinks. The group sat around telling tall tales of heroic rescues, wildfires and buildings that were saved by their dedicated efforts. The municipal workers told of massive undertakings that they had performed saving the community tens of thousands of dollars, and how their workmanship was far superior to the outside contractors that usually came down from Wilkes Barre or up from Allentown.

The time passed quickly and Mac instructed the fire fighters to douse the blaze so they could all go home – the rubbish pile had been reduced to a deep pile of smoldering ash.

The fire fighting team gathered and brought the hoses they had set up toward the rubbish pile. They opened the valves, the hoses expanded as the pressure built up, and they began laying water on the fire, which had calmed down and resembled a college fraternity bonfire in its dying stages. Great walls of hot steam and ashen gray smoke emanated from the pile mixed on occasion with acrid black smoke, which stunk like a truckload of burning skunks. The hot ash and unburned rubbish drifted up from the pile. The fire fighters killed the hoses and moved away from the pile.

The loader pushed the ashes that had drifted away back into the center of the pit. Some sparks drifted out of the pile and were doused by the fire hoses. Smoke began turning to steam, and the pile was periodically turned to ensure all the embers were out. The Assistant Chief circled the pit, taking notes and checking on the status of the fire.

The fire fighters were methodically quenching the remaining embers, when the young rookie called out to the Chief. "Hey Chief! Did you see that??"

The Chief replied, "See what?"

"I don't know! It looked like a shadowy figure made of smoke, a mean triangular face with wings on its back, and it sure didn't look happy!"

"Aw, the cider must have been sitting in the sun too long! If you're smart you won't tell anyone else about this – they'd most likely think you're crazy!"

The young fire fighter kept staring at the smoldering ash, still wondering if he really saw that shadowy figure. The figure he saw was clear enough that he could certainly identify it if he were to see it again. As the smoke turned to steam he saw it again, this time more dimly, but definitely the same figure, taunting him from the pit. It was an image he would never forget. He kept quiet this time – but he knew what he had to do.

It took about an hour to fully douse the pile, and when there was no more smoke and the Chief was certain the fire was out, the crew packed up their equipment, locked the gates, and left. After cleaning up the equipment and repacking their hose at the fire station, the fire fighters went home to their families, satisfied that the job was well done, and the landfill was ready for Memorial Day on Wednesday.

The young fire fighter kept thinking about the strange figure he had seen in the fire and decided to go with his instinct and discuss it with the Old Witch up on north Locust Street. Everyone called her "the Old Witch" because she ran a tiny establishment on the second floor of a rundown shop from which she told fortunes by reading cards and candle wax dropped in cold water. She sometimes did the horoscopes for the newspaper in Mount Carmel. Despite everyone in this small town knowing each other, no one knew the Old Witches real name, but everyone knew of the Old Witch. No one spoke of her or her shop and few were seen entering or exiting. She had a back door through which clients could enter who preferred not to be seen in her company. She held late hours and was open for business at 9 pm when the young fire fighter rang her bell.

The Old Witch opened the heavy solid wood door, which had a brass knocker in the form of some sort of a deity, its clenched hands pivoted around a plate bolted to the door, its feet were used to knock upon a brass plate, also affixed to the door. The big, old, solid wooden door creaked and groaned as it was slowly opened. Then, there before him stood the Old Witch. The young man stared at the Old Witch for a moment. Her face was haggard with age, but she was ageless. He could not even begin to guess how old she was by looking at her. She had a warm smile and a small round face around which lightly curled brown hair drifted aimlessly. In a light Ukrainian accent she invited the fireman in. The young man entered the shop, which resembled an early twentieth century miner's hut, only with all sorts of oddities sitting on warped wooden shelves and hanging from the ceiling. There were bags and jars full of odd looking spices, grasses and flowers and small tins and boxes full of incense. A human skull sat next to a black candle on a wide maple window ledge. There was one shelf filled with decorated Ukrainian eggs, some obviously chicken eggs, others much larger and a few were very tiny. All were adorned with images of far off places. Many were decorated for the holidays, mainly Easter and Christmas. One depicted the first thanksgiving, with the Pilgrims and Native Americans gathered around an open fire sharing supper from a communal table. They were all painted and inlaid with solid gold and silver filigree. Most were cut open and within the egg were tiny three dimensional dioramas. Several contained beautiful nativity scenes. All the eggs stood upon intricate gold, silver or glass bases, and some were carefully encased in glass boxes, bound together with silver banding. There were shelves full of dusty old tomes and on her small glass table sat a crystal ball on a silver stand, beside which lay an eerie black book with a bass relief of a horned god of some sort. There was next to it another book which was opened and he could see that each page was hand written and had odd sigils copied amidst the writing, all of which appeared to have been done by hand.

"What can I do for you son," the Old Witch asked.

"Well," the fire fighter began, "we were putting out a fire in the landfill today by the Odd Fellows cemetery." The boy paused.

"Well, go on!"

"Not so easy to explain. See, the fire was almost out and the smoke kind of drifted up, but it wasn't really like normal smoke. Kind of like an evil demon with a really mean look. It had wings, and crazed red eyes and an evil looking face. Its hands were claws with long sharp nails. I'd swear on my mother's bible what I saw but you're the only person I would ever tell for fear of being told I'm crazy. Do you think I am crazy?"

The Old Witch thought for a moment. "Well, it could be your mind was playing tricks on you, or maybe you really did see something. Now first, do let me know if you see or hear of anything else odd – I have had a few other folks come by with similar stories. It may well be that the devil has come for payment on our debt."

"What do you mean 'debt'?"

"Legend has it that many years ago the miners made a pact with the devil in an attempt to counteract the curse that the founding preacher of St Ignatius placed on this town back in the late

1800's. Just may be the old devil is coming to collect – you never get something for nothing, Getting in bed with Satan always comes with a huge price." She paused and picked up a small black bound book from her table. She opened the book and flipped through the pages, all of which were hand printed with hand drawn images. "Did your figure look something like this?" she asked, pointing to a figure in the book.

The young man's eyes glossed over with fear. He remained silent for a time. "Yes, that is exactly what it looked like!"

"That, my friend, is Beelzebub, one of the seven princes of Hell – a fallen angel, just like Satan himself. One of the most evil and fiendish beings of the underworld, and not someone you want to have to deal with. He has been called 'the lord of the flies' and was originally considered a god of the Philistines." The old witch became quiet. Although the various deities that have come and gone over time were well known, and she was a practitioner of witchcraft, a solitary hedge witch specifically, even to her these were fictional deities, or at best deities that were met in dreams and under the effect of hallucinogenic drugs and trances. Could it be that Beelzebub really exists? The boy, she pondered, certainly seemed to immediately identify the image he saw as that of Beelzebub. She concluded that this must be real and she would need to consult with others more knowledgeable in the history of the town and also those more familiar with this demon in particular. The Old Witch then reached up to a high shelf and retrieved a small purple cloth bag. "Now you take this as a gift from me – keep it with you at all times, and never look inside. It will keep you safe if the devil comes calling again. Now be on your way."

The young man accepted her gift and headed for home, more curious and concerned now than when he had arrived. He went home and his mother was waiting for him. She was curious how his day went with the fire company. He quickly changed the subject and asked his mother how her day had gone. He didn't discuss the demon in the fire with her, or the visit with the Old Witch, nor anything else that happened day.

The old man was becoming concerned about the time. His guests would be walking home in the dark, not something you want to do in a deserted town, haunted by the spirits of those who came before, and who have now been abandoned. "Folks, we're going to have to pick up the pace! I won't be able to tell you the fascinating story about the ghostly gatekeeper, nor all the issues that led to the condemnation of the town, but I do want you to understand why the remaining few are so desperate to remain in this desolate town. I am sure you have seen the armored vehicles, 4x4's and other 'unusual' equipment parked by some of the remaining homes – more like a military facility than family residences. Well, some folks don't believe in ghostly spirits and are more concerned about getting at the coal under this town. Hard to protect yourself from greedy capitalists."

The old man paused and rubbed his now cold pipe with his palm, as if summoning a genie. "You know, they thought that 'fire' was out, but that old devil is pretty darn stubborn. The firemen got a call two days later, the night before the Memorial Day celebration around 9pm. Darn landfill fire re-kindled! They would be in for a long night."

The birds began retreating for the evening, and several bats had come from their roosting in search of an evening meal. We all dug in and repositioned ourselves for the next chapter of this tale.

Chapter 10 – Landfill Cleanup Re-kindle

Town Landfill, Tuesday, May 29, 1962

George Jones, president of the cemetery trustees, was outside making sure the water tanks were filled for Memorial Day when he noticed smoke and flames rising beyond the eastern gate of the cemetery. He opened the massive iron gate and saw smoke and flames coming from the landfill pit. He immediately contacted Councilman Joseph Tighe who notified Councilman John May who notified the Mayor of the situation. The Mayor contacted the borough manager and apprised him of the situation. This was a major problem with Memorial Day less than 24 hours away.

It was about 8:30pm the evening of Tuesday, May 29 that the Fire Chief got the panicked call from the Mayor. He advised him that the fire at the landfill had re-kindled and was again raging out of control. The Chief assembled his crew and went with a couple of trucks to the landfill to assess the situation. With him was pretty much the same crew that had been present on Sunday at the burn. They arrived to an inferno in the pit, flames leaping into the air, and an acrid sulfurous stench everywhere.

The equipment was again set up to quench the blaze.

"How could this possibly have re-kindled to such a degree," the Fire Chief asked his Assistant. "There isn't even that much combustible material left in the pit!"

"Not possible, Chief, but it definitely is burning!" answered the Assistant Chief.

"Well either way, let's get it knocked down!"

The crew connected the pumpers to the hydrant on Locust Street and set up their equipment, staging a safe distance from the fire, but within easy reach of the water streams.

The crew began pouring water on the fire, but the fire only grew angrier. Flames reached dozens of feet into the sky and smoke was billowing out and began covering the town. Then, several monstrous flames reached skyward and moans could be heard coming from the pit.

"Chief! Did you see that!" exclaimed the Assistant.

"See what?" answered the Chief calmly.

"Those flames – they seemed to have eyes and facial features and seemed to be daring us to put them out! Even the smoke looks like evil demons flowing from the pit."

"You been drinking that tainted cider too? The kid saw something like that the other day – not possible, not worth ending up in the loony bin over either. Focus on putting out the fire, and put those visions out of your mind!"

From a distance the Old Witch watched as the men tried in vain to put out the blaze. She could see that something was not right. She could feel the evil even from where she stood. She could see that the flames did not look right. They seemed to be staring her right in the eye, daring her to challenge them.

Then the earth beneath them shook violently. "You are doomed!" moaned the very earth they stood on. The ground shook and trembled and a loud shriek arose from the pit. "Doomed... Doomed," the pit belched forth, as ash and cinders puffed up into the air, sparking and hissing as a crazed street cat. The ground shook a second time and two great fire breathing fissures opened before them.

"See!" said the assistant, "see! I am telling you, there is something in that pit!"

The Chief was no longer amused. Something was definitely going on here. "Quick, go get the camera in my truck," the Chief ordered.

The Assistant Chief returned with the 35mm camera, usually used to record fire scenes and automobile wrecks.

"Get as many pictures as you can – there's more film in the bag if you need it. We'll get this fire put out and have old Harry down at the photo shop print the pictures himself. Then we can have a closer look at what we are dealing with. The fewer people we get involved the better. Any idea who we can consult on this without looking totally insane?"

The Assistant Chief turned his head slowly and looked at the Old Witch standing on the hill.

"Are you insane?" the Chief queried.

"Chief, she's the only person who can even begin to understand this and who will definitely keep it in the house."

"Go get her and bring her down here, tell her what is going on and ask if she will help us. Go quickly!" the Chief ordered.

The Assistant climbed the hill to the cemetery boundary and approached the Old Witch. He explained what was going on and she recounted the visit with the rookie two days prior. She told the Assistant Chief that she, too, had seen the eerie figures in the fire and heard the voices from the pit. She accompanied the Assistant Chief to a safe spot with a good view of the fire.

The Assistant Chief told the Old Witch, "We'll meet at your place after we control this blaze if that is OK with you."

The Old Witch nodded in agreement, and the Assistant returned to the Chief.

It was now almost 10 pm and the fire was still unstoppable and had indeed become more intense. Water was not putting out the fire, and the odd figures continued to emanate from the pit. Every so often the earth would tremble and low toned voices or high pitched screeching could be heard.

"Chief, we need to get the borough manager involved. I think if we can push clay and sand into the pit we can douse the fire and stop this madness," the Assistant advised.

"Your thoughts are the same as mine. Go on back to the cemetery groundskeeper and ask to use his phone. This isn't something for the air waves. Get some heavy equipment and operators who can be trusted to keep their mouths shut!"

The Assistant complied, and now it was just a matter of waiting. The Assistant consulted with the Old Witch on their plan to control the fire and she agreed that this should plug the hole and put away the demons, but they would probably find a way to return. They would lurk underground, just waiting for a new mine shaft to open or an old one to subside and open up again. They were not going to go away by just burying them. No, they would need to find a more permanent solution to this dilemma or the town would surely be doomed.

The fire fighters continued pouring water into the pit.

The ground shook again and the pit moaned. The figures in the flames and smoke receded back into the pit, one by one. The earth shook lightly and the fire in the pit appeared normal.

It was midnight before the borough crew arrived with the heavy equipment; a cement truck and a large truck filled with sand.

Mac met with the Fire Chief. "OK boss, so what's the plan?"

"We drown the pit with four inch-and-a-half's so you can get your equipment in close. You drop the clay into the pit. Hopefully the fire dies and you can then dump the sand and cement."

"Hopefully?" Mac queried.

"Well, this is new territory for us. I'll fill you in later when I know more." The Chief didn't have time to try and explain the demons that were seen earlier. The fire now appeared to be a routine but out of control pit fire. No, best to see what shows up in the photos, and what the Old Witch has to say. Fortunately the demons had drifted back underground – for now.

The Chief motioned to his men who began dousing the flames simultaneously and Mac called to the dump truck driver to move in and dump his load of clay in to the mine shaft. Several other men were hanging on the driver's side of the truck which was shielding them from the heat of the blaze. As soon as they were close enough they jumped off the truck, pulled down the metal chute and began pouring clay into the pit. They stayed with the vehicle as it circled the pit dumping every last bit of clay.

The earth trembled and the flames and smoke receded into the pit. The sand truck followed behind dumping its entire load bit by bit as it followed the clay truck around the pit. The cement truck then dumped cement on top of the clay and sand. Water continued to flow into the pit from the fire hoses, taxing the Locust street mains. The hoses continued to play on the fire until no more fire, smoke or steam remained. It was almost 3am when the crew finally left the pit and returned home. The Old Witch agreed to meet with them Thursday, May 31 at noon at her shop. The Chief asked his Assistant Chief and the young rookie to come with him to that meeting, and asked the Assistant Chief to be sure and have the photos processed as well before the meeting.

The old man quickly re-lit his pipe, took a few puffs, and hastily continued with his tale. I passed out some "junk food" and water bottles I had brought along, as well as some more nutritious snacks, and we all repositioned ourselves as the story continued.

Chapter 11 – Debrief With The Old Witch

Thursday, May 31, 1962

Memorial Day was now history, and only a very select few knew the problems at the landfill that had to be tackled to achieve this perfect day. The wreaths were laid, the flags were planted, the little tents with goodies were packed up and all the memorial services were over. All the debris created had been moved to the landfill, and the town was clean as a whistle. The work days were back and the mail carrier was again delivering his mail and packages. The landfill was quiet and the town was happy. The flowers were in bloom and freshly planted flowers sat next to the graves of many good men who had fought and died in wars past so that we may live in peace and that our great nation may prosper. But, beneath the ground, evil still lurked. The fire kept burning, fanned by the evil demons determined to escape and wreak havoc on the small town that had conjured them so many years ago.

It was warm and sunny and was just about high noon when the Fire Chief, his Assistant and the young rookie fireman stopped by the photo shop. A few dusty old Brownie box cameras sat in the front window beside a beautiful Nikon F1 kit with a number of lenses, camera bag and tripod. Certainly not something any of the miners could ever afford, or would have need of, but more there to entice the curious into the shop to see what they could afford. Perhaps a Pentax K-1000? Or maybe just a 120 roll film Brownie box. This was a meeting place for the town. Young parents would bring in their films on an almost weekly basis to be processed and mine staff was always coming with film to be developed. Students would come to pick up their school pictures and to be photographed for prom and senior dance pictures. Then too, those on their way to foreign countries came for their passport photos. And then there was Jimmy, the owner. He was one of the most trusted people in town; after all he saw all the photos that came through his shop. He may well have known more about the townspeople than they knew about themselves. The townspeople knew he could be trusted with even the most intimate or explicit photos and some would ask Jimmy to process their photos in-house because of the controversial nature of the images. The only things Jimmy would not tolerate were images of illicit or illegal doings, and he had a sign up warning that such activities would be reported to the police, but aside from such images, pretty much anything else was allowed and everyone knew he would tell no one what he saw. And then, there were the images from the mine.

"Hey Jimmy, how did you make out?" the Chief said with an outstretched hand.

Jimmy firmly shook the Chief's hand. "Good morning Chief," he responded. "Got 'yer pictures done. Pretty weird stuff – I wasn't quite sure how to process these. Ain't never seen nothing quite so weird, 'cept in the movies." Jimmy handed a stack of 8x10 inch black and white photos and an envelope to contain them to the Chief.

The Chief rifled through the stack, passing the images to his Assistant who then passed them to the rookie.

"Yup!" the Chief answered. "I was kind of hoping the film would have been fogged, or just showed a big bonfire burning in a pit. Kind of hoping this had all been a bad dream, but I don't suppose that's the case. Jimmy, we're not certain what is going on here, but please keep this in total confidence."

"As always," Jimmy assured him. "Looks like you've got a weird situation on your hands. Hope it all works out, and if you need any help getting better images or just having your stuff processed, be sure and let me know."

"Thanks Jimmy. And expect Angie from the borough to be sending you a bottle of the good stuff and a check for your services."

The Chief shook Jimmy's hand again in thanks and the trio left the photo shop to consult with the Old Witch. It was just past noon and they were running late.

The Old Witch was just up Locust Street from the photo shop. They arrived around 10 past noon. Up the creaky steps they went to her second floor studio. They knocked on the heavy wooden door with the brass knocker. The Old Witch opened the door and admitted them.

"Good afternoon Chief; Assistant. Come in and have a seat by the glass table. And young one, we had a very long conversation, but we were never formally introduced. How may I address you?" the Old Witch asked.

"I am Tommy 'mam. Sorry for not introducing myself the other day, but I didn't want anyone to know I had come to you about this. Figured they'd all think I might be addled, seeing all those weird things in the fire and all."

"Oh that's OK," assured the Old Witch, "happens all the time. Well everything's pretty much out in the open now, so we can put all our cards on the table and try and figure out what's going on. How did you make out with the photographs Chief?"

The Chief pulled the pile of photos from the manila envelope Jimmy had put them in. The Old Witch viewed each, one by one, and then viewed them a second time. She said nothing, but dug through some old dusty volumes on a shelf against the wall, retrieving several large hand bound books with embossed images on the cover. One had an image of Baphomet that looked so real it seemed to be coming out of the cover and into our world. This volume was hand written with hand drawn images. It was almost 200 pages, all of which were filled. The Old Witch gently flipped the pages, looking at the photographs, then at the books. "You know Chief, Satan poses as many devils, some may call them demons or Satan's minions, but all are one in the same, Satan incarnate. One Satan becomes many devils, just as one God becomes many angels"

She returned to her books, found what she was searching for, and then turned the book so it faced the Chief. "See this Chief?" she began. "The triangular visage. The wings. The horns on the face and the wrinkled complexion. This is Belial. One of the most evil demons of the underworld. Even though I have been a practitioner of the black arts for many years I never thought these demons were real. Kind of like the Christian belief in God – the all knowing, all seeing, ever present God, who has no face and no presence but just is. But here, in this flame, is Belial. And we all heard the demon speak." She paused. "This is not good! This is very bad, and I am not certain even how to deal with this."

She returned to her books. She thumbed through them, page by page, and then she stopped again. "See. See. The horns. Shaped like a goat.

This is Baphomet. Baphomet represents everything, male, female, good and evil, all that is, all that was, and all that will ever be. Sometimes called the 'Sabbatic Goat.' History says that the Knights Templar worshiped Baphomet, but this is not true. This was a fable made up by the Orthodox Christian church to give them a reason to slay the Knights Templar and relegate them to history. Baphomet if he is real is not one to be fooled with."

The three remained quiet, intently listening to the Old Witch as she continued her research.

"And this. This is Abbadon, the one to be feared the most. His very name stands for destruction. He arrives on wings with multiple plates of impenetrable armor. He carries a sword looking like steel but unbreakable." She studied the images closer and pulled from a drawer a large glass with which to get a clearer view. "Can't make out any of the others," she said after a while, "but there definitely are several others, some in the flames, some in the smoke. I could feel them as well at the pit. I could perceive many demons, many more than are in these photos. If these evil spirits escape they could spread. They could take over and rule the world. Then not even your God could protect you, save the final chapter of the Holy Bible, Revelations; 'Hallelujah! Salvation and Glory and power belong to our God; because His judgments are true and righteous; for He has judged the great harlot who was corrupting the earth with her immorality, and He has avenged the blood of His bond-servants on her. And the fifth angel sounded, and I saw a star from heaven which had fallen to the earth; and the key of the bottomless pit was given to him. And he opened the bottomless pit; and smoke went up out of the pit, like the smoke of a great furnace; and the sun and the air were darkened by the smoke of the pit. And I saw a new heaven and a new earth; for the first heaven and the first earth had passed away.'"

The only sound heard for what seemed an eternity was the ticking of the large teak mantle clock, sitting atop a small case of books. Tick, tock; tick, tock; tick, tock...

Tommy broke the silence, "You mean what is happening in our small town could affect the entire earth?"

"Perhaps the entire universe," answered the Old Witch. "We need to find a way to seal the mines and lock the demons there for eternity. They need to be locked with a powerful spell that will hold them powerless. We will need the help of those far more versed in these matters than I am. There is a group in New Hope that we can consult with who work on the fringe. Perhaps we could have them on standby should the need arise. I know them quite well. They are very knowledgeable and may be able to provide some insight as to what is happening and how best to put an end to it. I will make contact with them and will get back to you as to what they suggest. In the meantime, should there be any other activity at the landfill be ready to get photos and record audio if you can. Anything you can find out and record will help."

The three agreed, thanked the Old Witch for her services, and left.

Saturday afternoon, June 2, The Old Witch made contact with a coven that worked out of a small home just outside of New Hope, PA. Raven Damiana introduced herself as the new High Priestess of the coven. The Old Witch had spoken with Elizabeth Octavian, the previous High Priestess, who turned over the reigns of the Coven after having been High Priestess for almost 10 years. Elizabeth was still an active participant in the coven. The Old Witch explained the situation to Raven and showed her copies of the photos. She explained that she heard the voices of the demons and felt the earth groan and rumble, and was truly concerned that this may be a breach of the Gates of Hell, and that the spell cast so many years ago may have transcended a simple conjuring and might become a serious issue to others. Raven agreed and asked the Old Witch to stay and meet with the coven later that evening.

The group of 13 and the Old Witch met around 7pm and after lighting four candles and asking for guidance from the spirits, proceeded to discuss the situation at the landfill in Centralia. The Old Witch was introduced to the others. She already knew Elizabeth. The last person she was introduced to was the youngest, just 20 years old. Her name was Tabatha Blake, and she was initiated just 6 months ago. Her parents had died a few years back in a small private airplane wreck. Her dad was a well trained aviator and held a private pilot license. He had flown planes in the Korean War, and was considered one of the Air Forces best pilots. Sadly, his small Cessna was not in the best mechanical condition. It suffered a malfunction in mid flight under less than ideal weather conditions and crashed, killing him and her mother. She had spent the past 6 months learning all the rituals and all the history of witchcraft. She was taught the seasonal holidays and how many of those correlate with Christian holidays. In times past, the Christian Church tried to assimilate the old Pagan holidays, perhaps figuring more Pagans would come into the fold through familiarity of the holidays. She also learned the mindset that is required to be a witch. Spell craft relies on powerful emotions, a strong will and a stronger desire to achieve results. It is really no different than diligent prayer. Witches she learned are truly misunderstood. They are not Satanists. They are merely practitioners of a different form of religion. The others in the coven put in many hours helping her to learn and to practice the rituals. She was a star pupil, and was truly dedicated and loved by all in the coven.

The group then sat on the floor on a large round mat on which was printed a pentagram in black. It was then that Raven noticed the pentacle necklace that the Old Witch was wearing. "That is really beautiful, where did you get that," she asked.

A pentacle is a pentagram circumscribed by a circle, and a pentagram is a five-pointed star that is formed by drawing a continuous line in five straight segments, forming a star. It is often used as a mystic and magical symbol of protection. The 5 points each have their own meaning. The upward point of the star is representative of the spirit. The other four points all represent an element; earth, air, fire, and water. When inverted, it is a Satanic icon. Most witches wear a pentacle of some sort, but the one the Old Witch was wearing was indeed unique. It was made of gold and platinum entwined around each other, the pentacle itself resembling the gnarled branches of an old tree. The edges were engraved with Hebrew characters.

"My grandmother made this herself over 50 years ago when she was living in the Ukraine. It has been a prized possession of mine since she gave it to me just before my family and I left for the United States. Sadly she died shortly after we left. We were unable to return for her funeral services."

"It is truly wonderful, and probably quite a powerful icon for you," Raven commented.

The group spent the next couple of hours listening to the particulars of the situation in

Centralia and deciding if this was something they wanted to take on. They first needed to determine if this really was a supernatural problem, or if all of the problems were just coincidental. Sometimes things are not as they appear. Our minds tend to create that which we expect and we are not always able to set our personal beliefs apart from reality. Certainly, the photographs seemed to provide proof of something terribly unusual going on at the landfill, and this helped to sell the plan to the coven. The 13 took a vote after Raven explained the dangers. The landfill area itself posed dangers. If demons really exist there, it could become extremely dangerous, perhaps beyond what they could control. Raven also told the group that the reason she feels they need to get involved is that if these demons are indeed real, which they seem to be, they could pose a threat to all humanity. Once they get a taste our world again, they could get greedy and begin causing havoc across the planet. Raven called for a vote, adding that they should only vote to take on the mission if they truly are committed and were willing to accept all the risks. All 12 voted to take on the mission. Raven sealed the deal by agreeing that she approved of the mission.

A plan was laid out for the coven to be on standby should the situation recur. Supplies would be at the ready and spells to secure the demons would be printed as well as memorized by the coven. The group would begin setting things up and practicing the spell casting immediately. This sort of work had not been done in recent times, and there would be much research to do, but the group was confident they could work up an effective spell to banish the evil spirits. The big question was, would it work in a real life situation, and could the town Mayor and council be convinced to allow it. And then, there was going to be the problem of locating the old texts describing the procedure to exorcise the demons. Iconographic documents relating to this kind of spell are quite rare, due to their being burned and hidden during the "burning times" when one could be tortured and burned just because someone told the authorities that they were a witch. Once found, any such document would need to be translated. In the old times many spells were translated to look like cooking recipes, where common cooking ingredients and processes were actually encrypted terms for other ingredients and procedures. This notwithstanding, Raven assured the Old Witch that even if they could not immediately put their hands on what they needed, there were many others, both local and in Salem, Massachusetts, who would be willing to help.

The coven gathered and closed the four gates and thanked the spirits for their guidance.

The Old Witch departed just after 10pm and returned home. She contacted the Fire Chief the next day and discussed the plan. The Chief assured her that should there be a recurrence there would be no problem obtaining the full cooperation of the Mayor and council.

All was quiet at the landfill with no sign of fire, smoke or demons up until the regular June 4th council meeting. The Fire Chief pulled aside the council president, the borough manager and the Mayor and showed them the photos and explained what was happening at the landfill. There was skepticism as to what actually happened, but the photos were pretty convincing. The Chief was given the go-ahead though, should anything odd recur at the landfill, to do what was needed, as long as it was kept quiet and out of the newspapers. The Chief agreed.

Chapter 12 – Fire In The Hole!

Tuesday, June 12, 1962

The phone rang at the fire station around 3pm. It was the Mayor. "Chief. I hate to tell you this, but that darn fire in the landfill is at it again! It just won't go out! Can you get your crew together and go down there and see what's going on?"

The Chief was distressed. This had to stop. "Yes Mayor," he answered. "We'll get over there right away. Keep it on the QT and we'll let you know how it goes."

The Chief called the same crew that had been used previously to put out the fires in the landfill. They debriefed at the fire station before proceeding to the pit. The Chief also called the Old Witch, and asked her to come as well.

When they arrived the pit was filled with acrid smoke. Bulldozer operator Charles Kasenych was already on the scene, stirring up the garbage so the firemen could douse the lower layers with water. Kasenych told the Chief the stench in the pit was horrible and the fumes made his head spin. The Chief asked what he found the conditions to be regarding the fire and Kasenych told the Chief that it was mostly smoldering, but sometimes when he pushed the garbage flames would leap up. The Chief requested that Kasenych pull back from the pit so the men could get in closer and get a better assessment of the situation.

The team once again began dousing the fire. The flames did not take on the demonic form as they previously had, but there were ominous rumblings under the earth.

The Chief held up the fire suppression to inspect the pit. The Chief then noticed that there was a large hole almost fifteen feet long and several feet wide at the base of the north wall of the pit near the cemetery. It had been concealed beneath the garbage and dirt and was not filled with noncombustible material. This hole led to an underground labyrinth of mine shafts, interconnecting many of the mines in the region. Perhaps they forgot to close this one hole, or perhaps it was opened after the fact. In any event, this was a point of ingress by which the garbage fire could take hold of the coal remaining in the mines. The abandoned shafts were the perfect breeding ground for the fire; great volumes of highly combustible anthracite, and great volumes of air. Later, council would deny knowing of this hole, and assured in its minutes that all mine shafts were properly sealed prior to opening the pit for waste disposal. A certification from a state inspection would confirm this. Perhaps the shaft was opened by the demons?? Time to meet with the Old Witch.

The Chief returned to his crew and advised them as to what he found. He called back the bulldozer operator and told him to get clay and sand and cement to plug the gaping hole. Perhaps this would smother the fire.

The Chief know this would only be a stop-gap until the real problem could be solved – that of the demonic possession of the town.

The Chief pulled aside the rookie and asked him to get the camera and the tape recorder and be sure to bring extra film and tape reels. The tiny reels of tape only held about 10 minutes of audio, and the Chief wanted to record as much of the fire suppression effort as possible. He also asked the rookie to pick one of the men to assist him. Tommy was proud that the Chief had trusted him with the authority to do this task and to choose his own assistant. He immediately set about the task.

The Chief pulled the Assistant aside and went up to the top of the hill on the north side to meet with the Old Witch.

"Thanks for coming here today," the Chief said to the Old Witch. "I don't think this is going to be the end of our troubles, and I strongly feel that if we plug the mine shaft today, in very short order the demons will break through, ever angrier by our efforts to stop them."

"I agree," replied the Old Witch.

"I think we need to bring the folks up from New Hope as quickly as possible and show them exactly what we are dealing with so they are prepared to act before it is too late."

"You are correct on all points Chief. They need to see exactly what we are dealing with and be able to plan accordingly. Are you prepared to put them up in a secure location and keep them away from pesky reporters?"

"Already have that covered. Farmer Millhauser has offered to put them up in the old farmhouse he just re-did. Plenty of room for them to set up and prepare before they take to the pit. Can you arrange it?"

"Consider it done," the Old Witch said as she turned and headed back to her shop.

The Chief and Assistant returned to the pit and ordered the men to commence fighting the fire once the hole was sealed. It took almost two hours for the borough staff to plug the hole with clay, sand and cement, and another two hours to put out the blaze. The rookie and his aid recorded and photographed the entire event, during which there were several rumblings and shrieks, and sound resembling voices, but which were not English words. Several wisps of smoke and a few of the flames seemed to have demonic form, but not like the previous fire. Still, the Chief thought, better to be safe than sorry. Even if it only takes a cleansing by the witches, so be it. May not get a second chance at this.

The next day the Chief was contacted by the Old Witch who said the coven from New Hope would be getting their gear together and would arrive Friday evening, June 22. They would all meet once the coven arrived at the shop of the Old Witch.

The Mayor also met that day with the Fire Chief to discuss the landfill.

The townspeople were growing anxious. Something had to be done, and quickly. A small group of concerned citizens had turned out for the June 4th council meeting and wanted to know what was going on at the landfill. The council replied – just the weekly trash burn. The crowd didn't seem to buy this. In a small town, everyone knows pretty much everyone and anything that goes on. This fire reeked too much of a cover up. And then, there were the news reporters who were beginning to get underfoot. Pesky rumor mongers. Give them the real story and they don't believe you. Don't tell them anything, and they will make up what they please, even if it is false, just to stir up the "real" dirt. The Mayor voiced concern over the plan to have a group of witches exorcise the town landfill. Seemed too farfetched, and if anyone got wind of this they would make a mockery of it. But the Mayor had a plan. He would set up a big town hall meeting for Monday June 25th, with free food for all. The meeting would be to discuss plans for the future and answer any questions the townspeople may have. It would be the perfect diversion. The coven could work in peace and the police would assist in guarding the landfill and keeping prying eyes clear of the area. The Mayor, being the direct supervisor of the police department, made them very loosely aware of the situation, sort of leaving out the part about the witches and the demons. The Fire Chief asked the Mayor if he wanted to be present at the meeting with the coven on Saturday, June 23, but he thought it would be better to remain distant of this operation in case he needed to run damage control should something go wrong.

The coven arrived, along with several family guests who offered to assist, and were set up in the old farmhouse. They would rest there until Saturday morning, at which time they would meet with the Fire Chief and the Old Witch. The Fire Chief and the Old Witch met with them. There were brief introductions and then Raven said they were looking forward to meeting at the Old Witches shop and perhaps acquiring some local trinkets to aid their exorcism. Raven asked where they could fill up their vehicles in the morning as the long trip had left them low on fuel. The Chief directed them to John Coddington's Amoco, pretty much the only show in town for many years. After making certain the troupe had all they needed for the evening the Fire Chief and the Old Witch left, looking forward to discussing the plan the next day and taking the coven out to see the landfill.

They all met around 1pm Saturday at the shop of the Old Witch. The room was crowded, but not too much so. The Old Witch held an occasional séance, in her shop, and she had all that was required to accommodate the group. The Old Witch had prepared a light lunch for the group, paid for the by the Fire Chief out of his budget. To hold down suspicions she had stopped by the local market and picked up supplies and prepared the meal herself, rather than have a platter prepared in advance.

The Chief brought out the photos and the audio recordings and went over the happenings of the past few weeks with the group. He also assured the coven that this operation would be kept from the eyes of the public and that the fire department would stand by at the ready at all times. He then asked Raven what their plan was.

Raven began, "It is one thing to exorcise a person, totally another to exorcise an entire town, especially a town that is beholden to such an evil curse. There is no precedence for such an exorcism. We are in new territory. We may drive the evil back, we may just provoke it. Our solution may be only temporary, or we may be able to totally cleanse the town. We can make no promises, only that we will do our best." She gazed upon a small glass case that hung on the rear wall of the shop. "May I see that?" she asked the Old Witch.

"See what?" asked the Old Witch.

"The old triskelion in your case."

The Old Witch took the silver triskelion, the triple overlapping triangle which represents "fate", from the case and handed it to Raven. "This was blessed by my great grandmother and handed down to me by my mother."

"May we borrow it for the exorcism?"

"If you think it will help, you certainly may, it certainly carries a lot of power with it!"

"It most certainly should!" Raven replied, eying the rest of her shop for anything that might be of use considering the local nature of the situation. "We will need some local coal, perhaps a few larger pieces, 8-12 inches or so, and also some local mining artifacts from around the turn of the century."

The Chief answered, "Not a problem, we will have them for you tomorrow!"

"What is the weather for Monday," Raven asked.

"Clear and warm, highs in the low 80's," the Chief said.

"Perfect." Raven pulled some ornate silver medallions from a large cloth bag she brought with her, each embossed with the King Solomon Pentagram. "Here, be sure and wear these on Monday, they will protect you from evil." She then pulled a tattered black book from the bag and flipped quickly through the pages until she came upon a drawing, a square inside a circle, with a word written in Hebrew on each side of the square, this surrounded by two circles, with more

Hebrew words inscribed around each. "We will need this drawn in heavy chalk by the pit. It must be about fifteen feet across. It is around this talisman that we will conduct our ceremony. This must be in place an hour before we begin."

"Consider it done!" assured the Chief, wondering to himself if he and his men could faithfully reproduce the characters in this sigil.

"Lastly," Raven added, "we will need 5 pillars, one at the center of the sigil and one at each of the cardinal points for the calling of the quarters. Each should be about 4 feet above the ground and embedded solidly in the ground. Each will hold a 5 inch pillar candle with a half inch wick."

"Also done!" replied the Chief. Now he was beginning to wonder if he had enough support staff to keep the area clear of prying eyes. This could get interesting, he thought.

Raven asked the Old Witch for a black candle. The Old Witch picked up a pillar candle, which sat upon a glass base, from a shelf and gave it to her. Raven placed the candle in the center of the table before them and lit it. "Let us all gather around and hold hands to ask for a blessing from the Goddess." They joined hands and Raven began, "Hectate, beautiful Crone of night, I call you here to set things right, Transform all the wrong and pain, And help to make this town whole again." She paused for a moment of silence and then added, "So mote it be!" This was responded in like kind by all the witches present. "Now, we need to confront the evil and see what we are dealing with. Let's get off to the landfill!" Raven concluded.

When they arrived at the landfill light wisps of smoke could be seen coming from the pit. Ash and dust surrounded the pit, and new waste had been recently dumped. The mine shafts were still sealed. This was a good sign. Raven wandered around the entire area and advised the Chief where they would need to set up. The Chief evaluated the area as well to see where he could stage the fire apparatus and personnel. The Chief jotted some notes on a lined yellow pad he had brought, and snapped some photos as well to add to his record. There was going to be much planning, and timing would be critical, both for the ceremony and so that as few people as possible would be present to witness the event. When they were all satisfied that they had a workable plan, they departed, with plans to meet Monday afternoon at the landfill.

The Old Witch returned to her store and pulled out a ragged old deck of playing cards. She had used these cards for many years to foretell the future for her clients. Her great grandmother had taught her grandmother who taught her mother who taught her how to use playing cards to foresee the future. In the Ukraine where her mother was born, divination was a common practice among the gypsies. It was one of their main sources of income, and they had to be really good at it in order to remain in business. Modern science tells us that divination is merely one's ability to ask questions and perceive subtle responses from the person whose fortune you are telling. And of course, many fortune tellers flat out cheat by going through purses, and listening in on conversations prior to the reading, etc. Then, there are the truly gifted fortune tellers, like the Old Witch. She is right most of the time. Heaven only knows how it works, but her readings brought out things known only to her subjects, and most of her predictions were spot on. Indeed, there were many people in town who would not let her read their cards, figuring that if their reading was not good, it was probably better not to know. And, in a small coal mining town, few people have a particularly stellar future in their cards to begin with.

The Old Witch mixed the cards, lay them down and lit a small white stub of a candle.

She quietly drew a circle in the air above her head with a small double edged Athame. Then, pointing the Athame to each of the small lamps affixed to the cardinal locations on the walls of her shop, she called the quarters, East, South, West and finally North. She planted the Athame in a small sand filled cauldron, grounding her spiritual energy. She then lit a small charcoal round, and placed upon it a few granules of cedar incense.

"Spirits of the most divine, I give to you this precious wine." She poured a bit of wine into a small glass chalice. "May this working be safe and true, and grant to me a clearer view." She laid a small glass mirror on the table.

She then began placing the cards on the table, one card at a time, as she had done many times in the past, asking the spirits to tell her the future of the town and how the exorcism would go on Monday. She rushed through the first laying of the cards, the past, the present, and other unrelated information, all of which was reading true as she turned up the cards. Then came the answer to her primary question. As she lay down the card, she turned ashen and she began to shiver. The five of spades. In its position it indicates losing a battle. She then laid the final card, the ultimate outcome card. Fear shown in her eyes. A tear rolled down her cheek. She pushed all the cards together, put them back in their box, and dumped them in the litter can on the floor, vowing never to read a deck of cards again.

Exactly what the Old Witch saw in those cards that day we will never know, but we do know the fate that was to come to Centralia, and this card most certainly reflected that fate.

The wind picked up and darkness was setting in. We were unsure if we were going to find out what happened that Monday at the Landfill. The old man placed a hand on the rock he had been sitting on, picked himself up and slowly stretched his legs. "Yes sir, the story sure does go on. I won't have the time to tell you all about the mine fire or the condemnation and evacuation of the town or the Gatekeeper or what happened after the demons were put back in then ground, but I will make sure you hear about what happened to those demons, and why the state left those last 7 structures standing and allowed the remaining residents to stay. Can't leave you hanging with no ending to the story!" He slowly sat back down on the rock, carefully repositioning himself as he prepared to conclude his story. We also repositioned ourselves, anxious to find out what happened in that pit.

The old man withdrew his pipe from his vest pocket, filled it one last time, waited for the wind to die down and lit it, cupping his hands around the bowl to keep out the wind. The pipe came to life and the old man smiled. "Yes sir! Some day that was at the landfill. Had a firsthand view of that from the top of the hill to the north. Made darn sure no one saw me either!"

Chapter 13 – The Exorcism

Monday, June 25, 1962 At The Landfill

The borough of Centralia has been operating a waste disposal area under permit number 443R issued by the Department of Mines and Mineral Industries.

In spite of all precautions to operate the waste disposal area within the provisions of the applicable law a fire of unknown origin started on or about June 25, 1962, during a period of unusually hot weather.

It now appears that the coal seams may have ignited resulting in a mine fire, the control of which is beyond the capacity of the borough to contain. It is therefore, respectfully requested that consideration be given by the Department of Mines and Mineral Industries to extinguish the mine fire as a project within its operations.

(Letter sent to the Department of Mines and Mineral Industries and signed by Mayor George Winnick and the borough council)

* * * * * * * * * *

Monday came and it was hot. It seemed much hotter than the 82 degrees that the thermometer on the barbershop pole read. It was the Pennsylvania humidity that made it feel that hot. Some say, it was hot enough to ignite the landfill. In any event, the Fire Chief got the call early that day that the landfill was again on fire. He would have to stall for time. The coven was not prepared – the plan was to be in place after the 5:30pm start of the meeting at the borough building. The Chief called a meeting with the Mayor, borough manager and the Chief of Police. The Fire Chief made a call to Raven to let her know what was happening and advised her that the plan was still on. He would find a way to stall for time. A small crowd had formed outside the landfill. The Police Chief spoke to the crowd and told them to attend the evening meeting if they wanted to learn more about the situation.

It was near noon and the Fire Chief began slowly assembling his crew and the borough crew, again with plans to plug the hole and quench the fire. This would buy some time to get the coven in place at a time when most of the town was occupied at the town meeting.

When the Chief got to the landfill he was shocked to see that not only was the mine shaft once again open, but the demons seemed to have returned, quietly taunting them as they arrived.

The Police Chief set a wide perimeter around the landfill, but this only made passerby more inquisitive as to what was happening. A press area was set up outside of any view of the landfill, but with the quantities of smoke being emitted by the landfill it was not possible to conceal the fact that the landfill was again on fire.

The firemen set up their equipment and positioned themselves at what they considered to be a safe distance, as previously planned. A borough crew was staged and at the ready to deliver, once again, the clay, sand and cement to plug the mine shafts.

Four fire hoses stood at the ready, awaiting the command from the Fire Chief to start flowing water. It was only 2 pm. The Chief insisted on another situational awareness review with his staff. He needed to stall a bit more. He and the Assistant wandered the perimeter taking notes and photos. They pushed aside the rubbish around the perimeter looking for hot spots. They measured the mine shafts which had opened and noted the size of the openings. The few onlookers must have wondered why they had not yet begun fighting the blaze.

A little after 3 pm the coven, accompanied by the Old Witch, arrived in a borough van. They were ushered to a safe area out of public view where they could begin setting up. The sigils and alter of coal were already in place, and the posts for the center and cardinal points were implanted where Raven had asked them to be.

The Chief gave the call to start flowing water. Trouble began almost immediately. The ground began to rumble, and the flames grew angry. "You cannot win," the flames shrieked. "You will all die in agony!" whispered the smoke. A long red forked tongue came from the largest flame and "kissed" the Chief, charring his leather helmet. "You too shall die!" the flame sputtered.

It was not possible to get near enough to fill the mine shaft as was done before. More time was needed. The demons had to be sent back into the pit before the fire could be put out. The Chief had his team begin flowing water into the pit, more for show than anything else, as the fire just laughed at their feeble attempt to extinguish it.

The ground made a loud grinding noise and a large jagged crack opened through the center of the pit. The burning waste dropped in, significantly reducing the height of the rubbish. The fire would now be much harder to put out, as much of the rubbish was now below ground and was burning furiously, having been agitated by the fall into the pit.

Outside the perimeter in the press staging area a reporter queried the borough press contact, "Did you hear that?"

The press contact replied, "Didn't hear nothing. You'll get a full report and a chance to get some photos once the fire is under control. Not safe to go into the landfill area right now."

The crowd, now more curious than ever, began migrating north up Locust to the town hall to find out what was going on and get the latest updates. Hopefully this would buy enough time to complete the exorcism. The coven was in position and ready to begin.

The Fire Chief called a halt to the flow of water, and the firemen backed off and stood ready to begin flowing again at the command of the Chief.

The 13 witches, dressed in long black robes, encircled the sigil on the ground and each held high a silver Athame. The Old Witch stood nearby in case she was needed, carefully absorbing and documenting the ritual. Raven began, "Lords of the Watchtowers of the East, Lords of air; I do summon, stir and call you up, to witness our rites and to guard the Circle!" She lit the candle on the south pillar and continued, "Lords of the Watchtowers of the South, Lords of Fire; I do summon, stir and call you up, to witness our rites and to guard the circle!"

There was a loud "BANG!" and the pit spewed forth a hundred plus tons of dirt and hot ash, spewing embers down on the witches. "Go away! You are not welcome here!" the ground belted out in anger.

Raven lit the west candle. "Lords of the Watchtowers of the West, Lords of Water, Lords of death and initiation; I do summon, stir and call you up, to witness our rites and to guard the circle!"

A huge flame, with what looked like bulging eyes and pointed teeth reached out roaring and crackling and smacked Raven on her left side, igniting her robe. The fast thinking rookie fireman quickly doused the flames with the booster hose he was operating.

Ignoring the danger, Raven calmly lit the north candle and continued, "Lords of the Watchtowers of the North, Lords of Earth, guardians of the Northern Portals; powerful God and gentile Goddess; we do summon, stir and call you up, to witness our rites and guard the Circle!"

The flames whipped wildly, the demon faces becoming ever more distinct. The flames were now almost independent of the fire and the smoke was dancing as if on feet. Surrounding the flames, shapes of demons made of smoke billowed high in the air, roaring laughter in deep intonations. The earth shook and the pit belched out more demons, and more hot ash and cinders.

This was the first circle to be sealed, there was yet another which would need to be sealed to protect the entire pit before the exorcism could be performed. But first, the deities had to be invoked.

The 13 joined hands and began circling the sigil widdershins. They chanted in unison, "We invoke and call upon thee O Mother Isis, who shines for all, who flows through all, Maiden, Mother and Crone. We invite you to our Circle.

Touch us, charge us, make us whole; we invoke and call upon thee O Father Osiris, Lord of the Sun, Master of all that is wild and free. We invite you to our Circle. Touch us, charge us, and make us whole. We pray you remain to save the day, and fix this town, and set it on its way!"

There was a loud thud and a whoosh and the rubbish shifted and started to slide into the mine shaft. "Go away!" the ground rumbled. The flames fanned a huge puff of smoke at the witches, who began choking and their eyes began tearing. "Go away!" They remained steadfast despite the warning and approached the center of the sigil to light the last candle, the candle representing spirit.

Back at the town hall the crowd was growing anxious. The borough council was stalling for time, preparing and presenting more food and drink and insisting they wait for any stragglers who might be arriving late from the mines. The crowd wanted answers. What is being done to put out the fire? Is it a mine fire? How did it start? Why does it continue to rekindle? Too many questions, too few answers. The crowd was seated and the Mayor began to slowly discuss the events at the landfill, excluding, of course, anything having to do with witches or demons.

At the mine, the witches returned to their original positions. Raven placed a large quantity of cedar incense upon a piece of hot charcoal. The smoke and wonderful cleansing smell of cedar filled the air. She picked up the large piece of coal she had obtained from the Fire Chief. "Hail to the Sun, God of Fire and Energy, whose light gives warmth and life to all beings. We ask you fill this stone with your bright energy, that we may use the power with harm towards none and for the good of all! So mote it be!"

"So mote it be," responded the other 12 witches.

"Stone of the Sun, You and I are as one. Your power is Mine and Mine is Yours. Together we work as one, our powers invincible, the demons are done! Blessed be. So mote it be."

"So mote it be," responded the others.

The pit was still flaming, the demons still present, but the voices were quiet, ominously so.

Raven, assisted by 4 others, lit 4 large torches and walked deosil around the sigil, planting each firmly between a cardinal point.

They stopped at their original positions and chanted in unison, "Power of Earth, Air, Fire and Water we have over thee! Power of good and evil, of lightning and thunder we have over thee! Power of the sun, the moon, the stars and all of the heaven's we have over thee!" They raised their Athames high and cut the air with a large "X" shaped pattern. The earth rumbled in protest and began belching smoke again. The flames rose high in the air, whipping wildly and banging haphazardly into one another.

It was then that all hell broke loose, literally. The demons were angry, they wanted no part of this and were determined to put and end this these rites. With one loud crash and a bang the flames and smoke came out of the pit and spread out over the entire landfill area. The acrid, burning scent of sulfur spread over the area. Hot ash and cinders fell and ignited anything they landed on. The burning hair and garments of the witches could be smelt. But the witches remained steadfast.

"Water! Water!" screamed the Chief frantically. "Man the hoses! Man the pumps!"

The water began flowing quickly into the pit. The fire engine pumps roared, giving every bit of water that was mechanically possible. Thousands of gallons a minute, but the flames just laughed at the weak human attempt to extinguish them. The 1952 Mack L fire truck pumps were screaming, pushing their 1500 gallons per minute through the two and a half inch cloth and rubber hoselines. They could push no more, and this was proving to be not enough.

"More water! More water damn it! The fire is spreading!" From behind a second fire pumper a soot covered black-faced fireman came running and shouting. "Around the other side! Quickly!"

Three more fire fighters joined in, sweat pouring from their brows in the humid 83 degree heat, the fire making the air many times hotter, dragging limp cloth hose toward the quickly spreading fire that was reaching out in anger from the pit. "Charge the line," screamed a scrawny teenage fireman. The hose they were carrying quickly began filling and whipped along like a disturbed snake.

This was a fire such as no one had seen before. A fire set and controlled by Satan himself. None of the locals had ever seen such an inferno. The flames leaping from the ground formed shapes resembling demons from Hell, the heat was melting fire apparatus staged many hundreds of feet from the pit.

A huge flame leaped from the pit. It displayed blazing arms reaching toward the ground. It had what looked like a wicked smirk on what seemed to be a fiery red face. It hissed and spat loudly throwing sparks hundreds of yards. There was a loud "whoosh" and a bang, and it was sucked back into the pit. The earth rumbled deeply from below. The rumbling became louder, an ominous warning of that which was yet to come.

A nun from the local Catholic Church clutched her rosary and prayed, "Lord God, save us from the evil we have unleashed!"

Out of the burning abyss came a thunderous roar, a fiery black belch like a volcano and smelling putrid of sulfur. Dust and burning ash again rained down from above. A black visage, vaguely visible through the smoke, floated in the air uttering evil in unknown tongues. Brilliant red flames in the shape of evil demons issued forth from the pit, their burning forked red tongues whipping wildly to and fro. A low pitched but quite perceivable reverberation could be heard warning, "Doomed! Doomed! You are all doomed!"

A blazing tail of fire roared from the pit and grabbed onto a police vehicle and two bystanders, dragging them screaming, slowly back into the pit with it, gone forever into the flaming abyss.

In the distance continued the rhythmic drumming, and the monotone sound of the group of 13 women chanting, "Guardians of the watchtower of the east, we do summon, stir and call thee to protect us in our rite. Come to us now on the cool breath of autumn's sigh which heralds the advent of winter and the close of harvest time. Breathe into us the spirit of the pure joy of life. So mote it be!"

There came another blast from the pit and the ground collapsed beneath a fire truck, sucking it down into the very bowels of hell, the ground closing over the vehicle and entombing it.

The circle continued, "Guardians of the watchtower of the south, we do summon, stir and call thee to protect us in our rite. Come forth from the cook fires and smokehouses where food is being made ready for the coming cold months. Kindle within us the flame of spiritual awakening. So mote it be!"

"Get back! Get back!" screamed a local police officer. "Move the perimeter back!!"

Quickly the entourage of fire fighters gathered their equipment, leaving behind the hose they had already laid, and pulled back to a safe distance. Local police circled the area keeping bystanders out of view of the inferno. The ground where they had been collapsed and all the equipment that had been left behind was swallowed by the earth.

The circle of 13, continued chanting and drumming, not missing a single beat, all the while moving more distant from the flaming hole.

"Guardians of the watchtower of the west, we do summon, stir and call thee up to protect us in our rite. Come forth from the rainbow hued morning dew that covers the fields, and is soon to be frost, that we may find peace of mind. So mote it be!"

There was a violent blast and a huge flame shot out from the pit, slamming into the young witch who had been closest to the pit. It was Tabatha. The flame set her robe on fire. She screamed, knowing this was the end, and a violent wind encased in black smoke dragged her into the pit and to her instant death.

The Old Witch calmly walked over to the circle and took her place. This was a terrible tragedy, but the witches knew if they stopped now, they would all be dead, as would all the people of the town, indeed, possibly all the people of our earth.

"Guardians of the watchtower of the north, we do summon, stir, and call thee up to protect us in our rite. Come forth from the fertile bosom of our Blessed Mother Earth, and nourish us so that our hopes may grow to fruition. So mote it be!"

Raven picked up a large cauldron of salt, "I exorcise thee, O Creatures of Hell, that thou return from whence you came; in the names of Isis and Osiris! Burn by this cleansing salt! Burn, and be burned forever! Never return to this town!" She then approached the fire and flung the salt in, her robe being singed in the process.

The wind picked up and the sky turned black, dark clouds forming quickly above the pit. Rain began pelting the ground, and lightning lit up the sky. Loud crashes of thunder rocked the earth. Raging flames leaped hundreds of feet into the air in anger and then dropped back into the pit. The smoke became blacker and more acrid and now began smelling damp, like a soggy rag that had been sitting in the rain.

Raven then picked up a bucket filled with holy water. "Damned be you and return to Hell, to dwell with the creatures of the night, with your Father Satan! Be damned for eternity! Back to the pit forever! Back to the pit!" In unison the 13 responded, "Back to the pit!" Raven approached the fire and dumped the holy water.

The earth groaned loudly in protest, the flames and smoke began receding into the old mine shaft. The earth trembled violently until the last of the evil flames and smoke were gone.

When the last of the flames had receded back into the pit Raven yelled to the Chief, "Quickly! Plug the mine! Plug the mine! Do it now!"

The Chief motioned to the bulldozer operator and dump operator. They quickly approached the mine shaft, all the while being doused by the firemen's hoses. Sand and clay were dumped and cement was poured on top, then more sand and clay. The Chief was determined that these evil beings were going to stay buried this time!

The 13 returned to the pit, dumping salt and holy water into it from small buckets that were prepared in advance. As they dumped this on the fire, the flames rose and fell in fits. The demons had been banished back to the underworld, for now.

The 13 reversed the calling of the watchtowers, banishing them and cleansing the pit, extinguishing the candles in order. They ended with the north watchtower. "Guardians of the watchtower of the north return now to the Earth where worms burrow deeper and seeds nestle awaiting the long sleep of winter. Take with you our blessings and our thanks. Hail and farewell!" In unison the 13 responded, "Hail and farewell!" Raven snuffed the last candle on the north tower. The 13 circled the pit 7 times, each carrying a censer burning dried sage, and then 13 times more carrying censers burning myrrh. They paused in silence to confirm their success and then departed the pit. The firemen moved their equipment closer to the pit.

The 13 witches then gathered just outside the landfill by the cemetary to mourn and say a prayer for their lost sister, wondering how they would explain to her remaining family what became of her. The Old Witch cried and apologized to Raven for bringing them to this God awful pit of Hell. Raven assured her that it was of their own free will that they came, fully knowing the dangers involved. The wonderful lady who perished will always be remembered for her courage and willingness to put her life at risk to save the many people of Centralia, and possibly the entire planet. They discussed the exorcism and agreed that although the demons were gone for now, someone would always need to remain guarding the pit, guarding the Gates of Hell so that the demons should not return.

The firemen continued dousing the fire in the pit. The borough staff finished plugging the mine shaft. The cleanup of the landfill continued into the night. The demons were gone, but now the fire had entrenched itself in the never-ending maze of interconnecting mine shafts. The town would end up dead, but the residents would continue to live, thanks to one small group of witches, determined to save the world.

Chapter 14 – The Road Home

"The difference between my beliefs and having a religious faith is that I am prepared to change my views in light of new evidence, but someone of a religious faith will just stick their fingers in the ears and say: 'I'm not listening, there's nothing you can say that will make me change my mind.'"
— *Jim Al-Khalili*

* * * * * * * * * * *

The winds had calmed, the stars were starting to show in a now clear sky, and the trees and all the living creatures were at peace. A light breeze was blowing from the west. It had turned cool. The tale had run much longer than we expected, but we savored every moment of it. We were still anxious to learn what happened in the later years, but this would have to wait for another day.

The old man sat quietly for a moment, observing the now darkened sky and the bats swooping low in search of insects.

"And that's the story," the old man said, returning his pipe to his vest pocket, there to sleep again until the next weekend. "The demons were gone, but the underground fire rages on to this very day and may well continue burning for another 200 years. Perhaps the demons are keeping it lit, or maybe it is just collateral damage. For certain though, those demons are still working on collecting that debt. If those mine companies ever come in and start strip mining this town they are sure to escape again, and after 50 plus years they'll be madder than ever! In any event, the state was forced to keep the few remaining residents to watch over the town, the landfill and the mine fire. To keep the demons buried, where they belong. Not even the powerful mine owners and their wealthy lobbies could convince the state to take over those last homes by force and give them the land to strip of its coal. Not when the destiny of the whole world could be at stake. No other good reason for them to give in and let the people stay."

The sun had set and it was now pretty dark, the birds were in bed and the bats had come out in search of insects to feed on, they fluttered above us in great numbers.

"You better be getting on now folks!" the old man continued. "Just mind your distance from the Gatekeeper, and if you see him, don't look into his eyes, lest you become possessed of him. And if you come back sometime I can tell you all about what happened during the 50 years from 1962 to the present, and maybe I'll even get to tell you the story of the Gatekeeper!" The old man turned around and began walking up the old Route 61. We turned for a moment to get our bearings and when we looked back to say goodbye, the old man was gone.

We started back, retracing the path we took to get to the highway. We trod again over the many slogans chalked by time forgotten hands. Back over the grass filled cracks in the highway. Past the utility poles with wires coming from nowhere and leading to nowhere, never again to carry power or telephone conversations. Past many large trees, bending over the road from age.

Beneath a gnarly old bush off to our left was a couple, entwined in forbidden love, oblivious to our passing. As we continued down the road the dirt bikes and 4-wheelers zoomed past us, they too were returning home. The old man and woman with the canes too short to be of use, greeted us with glee, happy to have found the graffiti riddled highway after paying a visit to the cemetery. We also passed the young couple who had asked us about the highway. They had finally arrived after making a number of overlapping side trips. They seemed pleased nonetheless that their scrappy piece of paper with the unintelligible instructions eventually brought them here.

Back through the narrow opening between the two large trees we went, getting back on the dirt road leading to the St. Ignatius cemetery. The bunnies and playful squirrels were gone now, and fuzzy, unrecognizable, fast moving creatures had taken their place, scurrying this way and that. The trees waved slowly back and forth in the cool summer breeze. Then we came upon the St. Ignatius Cemetery, its gates were still ajar. That's when we saw him. A shadowy figure in the darkness, surrounded by a faint purple halo. He was slowly coming out of the darkness from between the trees and a now long deserted road. It was the Gatekeeper, headed toward the massive gates of the St. Ignatius Cemetery. He was dressed in black from head to toe, his head being covered by a pointed hood. He walked slowly and deliberately, one step at a time, as though not by conscious control, but rather by rote in a programmed fashion. Though we were told not to do so, we couldn't help but look at his face. All that we saw was a black void. No eyes, no face, just black where all his features should have been. He ambled slowly toward the gate, unlocked the big steel lock, removed the chain, and closed the gates with a loud clang. He wound the chain around the now closed gates, clamped on the lock, turned, and returned the way he came, step by step, into the darkness, vanishing before our eyes as if into another dimension.

John and Tyler doubled their pace, and Anna and I were unable to keep up, despite our short legs working double time. After a bit we could only see the dust coming from the heals of their shoes in the distance.

We again passed the area left barren by the fire, passed the few wisps of smoke weeping from small cracks in the dirt and rock. Back over the roads to nowhere, and eventually back to John's truck where John and Tyler were patiently waiting for us. Both were panting from exhaustion and were sucking smoke from almost finished cigarettes. We all quickly got into the truck, headed for the highway and left Centralia for home. The ride home was quiet. Unusually so. We were all deep in thought.

Had we really seen the old man with the worn out pipe and tattered clothes, who vanished mysteriously into the dark? Did we really see the eerie Gatekeeper who seemed to have no face? Had this all been a dream? Was the old man's tale true?

We may never know the answers to these questions, but having been to this now desolate piece of earth, where only the dead and a few old stragglers remain, our hearts and prayers go out to all those who were forced to leave their homes and hope that they, and their descendents may find happiness; and that the souls of the long departed, residing forever in the cemeteries of Centralia may rest in peace.

* * * * * * * * * * * * * * * * * *
Dedicated to the town of Centralia
And all its former residents
* * * * * * * * * * * * * * * * * *

Did you enjoy this book?
Please stop by amazon.com and write a review.
Just search "Centralia PA" on Amazon to find the
book.

Andrew Shecktor